Praise for

THE DOOMSPELL

'... a vivid world of magical possibilities in which children discover they have amazing powers' *The Times*

'High fantasy, richly imagined, and refreshingly well-written' *Sunday Times*

'Gripping ... racy ... children have been fighting to borrow it' *The Guardian*

'A magical read ... *The Doomspell* never fails to enthral and captivate' *Amazon*

'... brilliant, breathless and filled with action from page one. If you want a book that you can't stop reading this is it. Enough talk – just read!' *Kids Out*

'*The Doomspell* is a perfect example of a great new voice in writing for children. This is a closely written and exciting fantasy novel that has all the elements to make it a bestseller ... McNish has created an incredible world in which the reader will become totally absorbed' *The Bookseller*

'A thrilling and magical read ... full of brilliant descriptions of events, characters and places.'
Library and Information Service for Schools

'Places him firmly among much more well-known names such as Philip Pullman and C.S.Lewis — Ithrea is a truly complete world, and the characters are beautifully conceived to obtain an emotional response from the reader.' *BookMonster*

By Cliff McNish

The Doomspell Trilogy

The Doomspell
The Scent of Magic
The Wizard's Promise

The Silver Sequence

The Silver Child
Silver City
Silver World

FOR OLDER READERS

The Hunting Ground
Savannah Grey
Breathe: A Ghost Story
Angel

FOR YOUNGER READERS

Going Home
My Friend Twigs
The Winter Wolf

THE DOOMSPELL

Cliff McNish

DOOMSPELL
BOOKS

First published in Great Britain in 2000 by Orion Children's Books
Paperback edition first published in 2001 by Dolphin Paperbacks
Reissued in 2008 by Orion Children's Books
Reissued in 2012 by Hodder and Stoughton
Reissued in 2017 by Doomspell Books
This edition published in 2018 by Doomspell Books

9 11 13 15 14 12 10 8

Text copyright © Cliff McNish, 2000
Illustrations copyright © Geoff Taylor, 2000

The moral rights of the author and illustrator have been asserted.

*All characters and events in this publication, other than those clearly
in the public domain, are fictitious and any resemblance to
real persons, living or dead, is purely coincidental.*

All rights reserved.
No part of this publication may be reproduced, stored in
a retrieval system, or transmitted, in any form or by any means,
without the prior permission in writing of the publisher, nor be
otherwise circulated in any form of binding or cover other than that in
which it is published and without a similar condition including this
condition being imposed on the subsequent purchaser.

A CIP catalogue record for this book
is available from the British Library.

ISBN 978 0 9955821 2 5

Printed and bound in Great Britain
by Clays Ltd, Elcograf S.p.A.

www.cliffmcnish.com

For Rachel, of course

contents

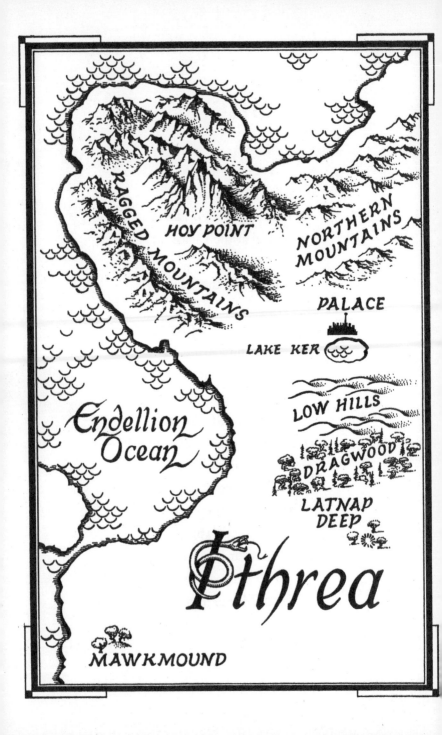

1

the witch

The Witch descended the dark steps of the Palace. It was a freezing night. Snow blew wildly in the sky and the wind howled like a starving wolf.

'What a delightful evening,' sighed the Witch happily.

Despite the bitter cold she wore only a thin black dress and her feet were bare. A snake clung passionately to her neck, occasionally blinking ruby-red eyes through the snow flurries.

The Witch walked effortlessly, relishing the crunch of ice against her toes, while a man alongside struggled to keep up. He was less than five feet tall and over five hundred years old. Bow-shaped creases either side of his eyes made them appear as if they had been gouged out and re-inserted many times. He shuffled down the steep Palace steps, only a big, flat nose and square chin exposed. His scraggy beard was neatly tucked under three scarves.

'Well, how do I look, Morpeth?' the Witch asked.

She flashed a pretty-woman face.

'It will convince the children,' he muttered. 'Why bother

to make yourself look nice, Dragwena? You don't normally care what they think.'

The Witch reverted to her normal appearance: blood-red skin, tattooed eyes, the four sets of teeth, two inside and two outside the writhing snake-mouth. Morpeth watched as the rows of teeth snapped at each other, fighting for the best eating position. A few purple-eyed, armoured spiders swarmed between the jaws, cleaning the remains of her last meal.

'Ah, but tonight a special child is arriving,' the Witch said. 'I don't want to frighten it too soon.'

Morpeth made his way down the remaining icy steps of the eye-tower. It was the highest point of the Palace, a thin column piercing the sky. Below, the other jagged Palace buildings huddled in the snow, their black stone poking up like beetle limbs. Morpeth placed one foot carefully in front of the next. He preferred not to slip – if he fell the Witch always waited until the last possible moment before rescuing him. Tonight he noticed Dragwena was unusually excited. She gently rolled the spiders on her tongue and laughed. It was an ugly laugh, shrill, inhuman – like the Witch herself. Through nostrils shaped like slashed tulip petals she sniffed the air eagerly.

'A perfect evening,' she said. 'Cold, darkness, and the wolves are out. Can't you smell them?'

Morpeth grunted, stamping his feet to keep warm. He could not smell or see the wolves, but he did not doubt Dragwena's word. Her bone-rimmed, triangular lids opened and stretched backwards under her cheekbones. Every detail of the night was always clear to the Witch.

'And the best of the evening is yet to come,' she sighed.

'Soon new children will be arriving. No doubt they will be the same as always – a little puzzled, yet grateful to receive our care. What will we do with them this time?' She grinned, and all four rows of teeth thrust forward menacingly. 'Shall we frighten them to death? What do you think, Morpeth?'

'Perhaps they'll be useless,' he replied. 'It is a long time since a special child arrived.'

'I think tonight will be different,' said the Witch. 'I have sensed this one for some time, growing in power on Earth. It is gifted.'

Morpeth did not reply. Although it was painful to spend any time in the Witch's company, tonight he wanted to be at her side. If a special child arrived he desired to know almost as much as she, but for different reasons.

They continued to descend the eye-tower. At the bottom a carriage awaited, led by two nervous black horses. The Witch usually flew to greet new children, but on a whim she had decided against it this evening.

Impatiently she watched Morpeth totter down the last few steps. So slow, she thought. So old. It would be enjoyable to kill him soon, when he was no longer useful.

Pushing Morpeth inside the carriage, she whispered a spell of panic to each horse and they bolted in terror towards the Gateway.

2

the cellar

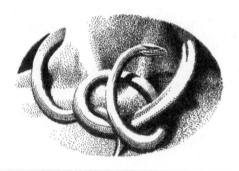

'What's the matter?' Eric asked, munching his cornflakes.

Rachel shrugged. 'You know.'

'The dream again?'

'Mm.' Rachel allowed her long black hair to dangle close to the breakfast milk, then flicked it at her brother.

'Leave off,' Eric said. He pressed his face close to Rachel, opened his mouth wide, and let milk and cornflakes dribble over his grinning lips.

'Oh, grow up,' said Rachel.

Eric laughed. 'Grow up like you? No thanks.'

Rachel ignored him, staring at her untouched plate.

'The dream changed last night,' she said. 'This time there were—'

'Kids,' Eric finished. 'I know. I saw them. In the snow behind the woman.'

Their mum stood nearby, stirring her coffee. 'Not that

again,' she sighed. 'Look Rachel, you began this dream rubbish. Now Eric's at it too. I wish you'd just drop the joke. It's not even funny.'

'Why don't you believe us?' Eric asked. 'We're both having the same dreams. *Exactly* the same dreams.'

'Last night,' said Rachel, 'the kids were shivering behind the woman. They had big creases around their eyes. They were covered in frost.'

'They looked half dead,' Eric said.

'Oh, stop it, both of you,' their mum warned. 'I'm fed up with all this nonsense.'

'I'm telling you, Mum,' said Eric. 'The woman in the dream's weird. Dark snow falls around her head. And she's got a snake-necklace. It looks right at you.'

'It's alive,' said Rachel.

'You've been practising this routine,' their mum said impatiently. 'I know you two. Do you think I'm daft? Get on with your breakfast.'

Rachel and Eric fell silent, finished eating and left the table. It was Saturday, so they could do what they liked. Eric trotted down to the cellar to play with his model aeroplanes. Rachel, deep in thought, went to her room to read, hoping it might take her mind off the dream. How could she convince her mum they were telling the truth? After a while she glanced up to see her mum standing hesitantly in the doorway. She might have been standing there for some time.

'Look, are you serious about this dream stuff?' she asked.

'Yes.'

Her mum glared. 'Really?'

Rachel glared back. 'Mum, I wouldn't make anything like this up. They're not like normal dreams.'

'If you're pulling my leg—'

'I'm not. I'm telling the truth.'

'Mm. All right.' Her mum rattled a bag. 'I'm going shopping. We'll talk about these dreams properly later. Where's your dad?'

'Have a guess, mum.'

'In the garage, fixing the car.'

'Again,' said Rachel.

They both laughed.

'Keep an eye on Eric for me, will you?' her mum asked.

Rachel nodded. 'OK, I'll check on him in a bit.'

Her mum left and Rachel turned back to the book, feeling much happier that someone apart from Eric was starting to take her half-seriously about the dreams. Outside a few cars zoomed by on the street. Some giggling kids ran past the house, setting off next door's dog. Dad cursed a couple of times from the garage – the typical Saturday morning sounds. Eventually Rachel yawned and went to find Eric. She made her way along the upstairs corridor – then stopped.

What she heard was not a usual Saturday morning sound. It was a scream.

Where from? Below her, yes. But not the kitchen, or the living room. 'Eric?' she called, listening carefully. There was definitely shouting. It came from the depths of the house. As she neared the cellar Rachel's shadow flickered orange against the wall. A fire?

'Get off!' Eric's voice roared. 'Someone help! What's holding me against . . . let go of me!'

Rachel reached the wide-open cellar door. She sniffed the air cautiously, peering down the steep flight of steps.

Inside there were no flames, but the entire cellar throbbed and blazed with crimson light. It was as if a great sunset had grown tired of the sky and burst into the house. Rachel shielded her eyes. On the wall at the back of the cellar a large black shape thrashed in mid air. She gasped, falling to her knees. Where was Eric? She could hear him panting. She followed the sounds and realized that the black shape *was* Eric. Both his feet flailed, his body pinned to the wall.

'Rachel!' he bawled, seeing her. 'Something's holding me. I can't get loose!'

She ran down the cellar steps. 'What is it?'

'I don't know! I'm stuck! I can't see it!' He thumped the wall behind him. 'C'mon, get me off!'

She grabbed Eric's wrists, pulling hard.

Then Rachel saw the claw.

It was an enormous black claw, the size of a dog. As Rachel watched it sliced through from the other side of the cellar wall. The claw gripped one of Eric's knees. It spread across his leg and yanked it through the bricks, outside the cellar.

'What's going on?' Eric wailed, noticing Rachel's wild expression. 'Can you see it? Don't just *stand* there!'

A second claw poked through the bricks. It encircled Eric's neck with three ragged green fingernails, wrenching his head completely through the wall.

Rachel leapt forward. She seized one of Eric's arms and heaved, inch by inch drawing his neck and face back into the cellar.

'Pull harder!' Eric's muffled voice yelled. 'Find something to fight it with!'

Rachel's eyes darted about for anything sharp. But whatever lurked beyond the cellar was not about to let Eric escape. The black claws again smashed through the wall. This time they stretched towards Rachel. As she backed away, the bony fingers hovered in front of her face and slapped her *hard.*

Rachel fell – and lost her grip on Eric.

Instantly, both claws tightened around his waist. They dragged Eric completely inside the wall. For a moment one of his arms shot back into the cellar, his nails scratching the floor as he tried to hold onto something, anything – before that was ripped away too.

Rachel staggered back, shaking violently. A loosened brick dropped near her feet, but there was no sign of the claws. She wiped a sleeve across her bleeding lip.

Get . . . Dad!

She retreated up the cellar steps, never taking her eyes off the wall. At the top she twisted and lunged for the door.

It slammed shut in her face.

Rachel reached for the handle, and yelped – it was too *hot* to touch.

Then, behind her, there was a ferocious rasping noise. The back wall heaved and tore open. Bricks burst like splintered teeth on the floor.

Rachel, shielding her hand with her jumper, tugged hard again.

'It's stuck tight!' she screamed, banging against the door. 'I can't open it. Dad! Dad!'

A blast of wind smashed her back. Rachel spun around. She saw that a *new* door was growing inside the back wall of the cellar. It was no ordinary door. It was luminous green, shaped like an eye, and slowly widening. A large black claw, the same giant fingers that had slapped her across the face, dragged it open.

Rachel heard dull thuds above her head.

'Dad!'

'Who's in there?' he said. 'What's all the racket about?'

'It's us – me and Eric! We're . . . something's trying to get in!'

'I can't hear what you're saying,' he bawled. 'What's that noise in there? What kind of game are you—'

'We're shut in! Dad, help us!'

He started pounding on the cellar door.

Immediately, as if sensing his presence, the wind slicing through the eye-door became a raging storm. It tore at Rachel's head, picking up all the cellar dirt, throwing it into her eyes. A wooden stool slithered across the floor. Eric's model aeroplanes spun crazily in the air, smashing over and over into the ceiling.

Rachel could barely breathe. The wind drove like fists, clogging her mouth and nose with dust. Dad could no longer be heard.

'Where are you?' she shrieked.

Suddenly, there was a splintering sound – an axe tearing into wood.

'Hold on!' Dad bellowed. 'I'm coming!'

Rachel felt herself being dragged backwards. She pushed her feet against the cellar steps for grip, clinging to the door frame with her fingertips. Dad's axe cut repeatedly through the door, but it was too solid to break down. He dropped the axe, thrusting his hand through a slash in the wood.

'Hold onto me, Rachel. Don't let go, no matter what happens!'

She caught his wrist. Then, blinking away the grit hurting her eyes, Rachel made herself look back. She saw that the eye-door now covered almost the entire back wall. Two claws stretched it open, and between the claws, filling the space, was a vast black creature with triangular green eyes. Hair all over its body bristled in the wind. On the tip of each hair a tiny serpent's head sprouted. The snake-heads seethed forward into the cellar, trying to bite Rachel's legs. Rachel tucked her knees in, kicking out, still clutching Dad's hand.

The creature within the eye-door was trying to push its way inside, but it was still too large to enter the cellar fully. Then, for the first time, a gaping mouth opened in the middle of the creature's head. Inside the mouth, between four sets of teeth, a dozen purple-eyed spiders rushed out. They crept along the body hairs towards her.

The mouth whispered, '*Rachel . . .*'

She screamed and, just for a second, let go of Dad's hand.

That second was all it took.

Immediately, the storm picked her up and yanked her through the eye-door.

The black creature lowered a shoulder to let her pass. It took a last look around the cellar. It sucked the spiders back into its mouth. The last image Rachel saw before she left this world was its huge shadow pass underneath and Dad smash down the main door with the axe, leaping through the air.

He was too late. With a final screech the cellar bricks reformed and the creature pulled the eye-door shut.

Rachel's dad ran into the cellar, beating his hands against the wall. Pieces of falling furniture crashed against his head. He ignored the pain and heaved the axe into the wall over and over. Eventually, when he had no strength left, he let the axe drop. The only damage to the wall was a few chipped bricks.

He stared furiously at the hand which had lost Rachel's, kicked the axe across the floor of the cellar, and wept.

3

Between
the Worlds

The moment she was sucked through the eye-door, Rachel found herself plummeting inside a vast, dark pit of emptiness. She covered her face, waiting to be crushed. Instead, she simply fell endlessly in the darkness, tumbling for several minutes, barely able to breathe as a freezing wind tore at her head.

Then, as if a cushion had been placed beneath her, Rachel came to an abrupt stop. Her body hung suspended in space, swaying gently. All around the air was still dark, but now Rachel noticed something even more densely black gripping her arm – the cellar creature. For a moment its triangular eyes, each the size of Rachel's face, held her in a fierce gaze. Then it pushed away, its immense shapeless body disappearing below.

As soon as the creature released her Rachel fell headlong again.

After several agonizing seconds she forced herself to stop screaming. Without consciously thinking about it she put her arms outward, cupping the darkness. Her spin slowly came under control, until she could tell she now only pointed one way – straight down, feet first. She thrust her shoes flat against the air below. *Slow down,* she thought, drilling into the air like a skier into a slope. She kept that idea alone in her mind, until the blasting cold air became a gust and the gust merely a light breeze rippling against her head and shoulders.

She concentrated, and said, 'Now, *stop.'*

As if the air around her had been waiting to hear this command all along, her body lurched to a dead halt.

Did I do that? Rachel wondered. How could I have done?

She told her body to turn slowly. Instantly it obeyed, revolving in a perfect circle, allowing her to peer around. Rachel gasped, bewildered. She lifted her hand. It stood so close to her face that she could feel her breath on it, but in the darkness it was invisible. Let me see it, she thought. Immediately, her hand gleamed dimly a few inches in front of her eyes. Rachel gazed in wonder, wriggling her fingers. 'The rest,' she said out loud, and her whole body lit up dully. Brighter, Rachel thought, and her body became a torch in the utter blackness around. *'Light up everything,'* Rachel shouted. She expected the space around her to burst into bright colours. Instead, all remained dark except for millions of dust motes shining close to her body, streaming upwards with the breeze.

She trembled. How could these incredible things be happening? She felt an exhilarating strength inside her, of powers strange and unrevealed, waiting to be used. What could it mean?

Rachel studied her surroundings. She hung inside a dark, fathomless silence. There were no walls or ceilings, no way to tell how far she had fallen or how far away the ground might be. Moist air from below streamed gently through her hair. Eric was nowhere to be seen. She tried calling – the breeze took her faint voice up and away. There were no other sounds.

Rachel's lip swelled where the claws had struck her in the cellar. A small drop of blood trickled down her chin and rolled off the end. Squinting, she could just make it out for a few seconds as it rapidly fell away.

There had to be a way to find Eric . . .

'Where is he?' she asked the darkness and immediately, below her feet, she saw a twisting blue dot. She *knew* that colour – Eric's jumper. 'Bring him to me!' she ordered – but this time her command was not obeyed. The blue colour merely dwindled, falling further away every second. The creature must be out there somewhere, Rachel knew, perhaps fixing its triangular eyes on Eric. Did he have her skills, or was he just tumbling over and over, terrified?

Fighting her fear to go downwards at all, towards the creature, Rachel knotted up all her courage and told herself to *dive* towards the faraway blue. Her stomach twisted. The next moment the wind whipped her head back and Rachel hurtled down. Faster, she told herself, and her body obeyed, the warm wind turning to frost against her face.

*

Ahead the blue shape loomed closer. Rachel swooped, using her arms like wings, and fell alongside Eric. She caught his spinning body and brought them both to a stop. Eric was unconscious. The fall, or fear of falling, or the wind driving out his breath, had made him faint. For a long time she hugged Eric until he awakened, and then she let him cry deeply into her shoulder, soothing him. For several minutes he lay cradled in her arms, while she murmured gentle words and sounds, allowing him to recover. At last he turned his face sheepishly towards her. A trail of sick hung from his mouth, plastering his neck.

He stared at her. 'You're . . . *shining*, Rachel. What's – happening?'

Rachel raised her eyebrows. 'I don't know, but while you've been out cold I've been experimenting. Watch this.' She focused her mind, turning her hair red, then yellow, then back to black.

'H-how'd you do that?' Eric stammered.

'Not sure,' Rachel said nervously. 'But I haven't found much I can't do.' She made her lips glint gold.

Eric blinked several times. 'Can I do it?'

'Try,' said Rachel. 'Just tell part of you to light up.'

Eric screwed up his eyes in concentration. His lips did not glow. He tried several more times, without effect. Eventually he gave up. 'What's going on?' he asked seriously. 'We're heading for the thing that dragged us in, aren't we?'

'No. We're just hovering here.' Rachel gingerly licked her sore lip. 'I suppose we should try to go down, though. We can't hang around here forever.'

'Don't go down, you idiot,' Eric said. 'Fly up, Rachel! Take us back to the cellar.'

Of course! Why hadn't she thought of that? Rachel clutched Eric and imagined them both cruising into Dad's arms. Nothing happened. She tried shoving herself up only a few feet. Still nothing.

'Great,' Eric moaned. 'I suppose that thing wants us to hang around.' He peered mournfully below. 'Did you see it? I know it was big.'

Rachel told him what happened in the cellar, missing out the part about the snake-hairs and spiders.

After a long silence Eric said, 'If it followed you down here, it's probably waiting at the bottom.'

'Maybe.'

'Definitely.'

'Mm.'

With no way to fly upward, Rachel allowed them to slowly descend. For a few minutes they both stared anxiously into the gloom, expecting the black claws to reach out of the dark.

'Hold on!' blurted Eric at last. He pointed to a weak spot of light below. 'There's something down there. It's coming towards us. Look!'

Rachel gazed in the direction of his finger, where a tiny grey patch, growing rapidly wider, formed beneath them.

Eric said, 'The thing's black, isn't it?'

Rachel nodded. 'With green eyes.'

'Maybe it's not black now.'

'It could be someone else dragged here with us.'

'Too big for that,' Eric said, matter-of-factly.

Rachel saw he was right. The grey object drew closer, spreading out to cover the whole space below. It was not another child. It was vast and featureless.

'It looks soft,' Rachel said. 'Don't you think so?'

Eric began kicking the air. 'We're going to hit it. That *thing*'s down there! Stop us moving!'

Rachel tried to do so, but they just continued to drift towards the greyness. At last they fell so slowly that a feather would have passed them. A chill touched Rachel's skin, followed by a freezing gust of wind. The surrounding air was not only colder, but studded with points of winking light.

'They look like stars,' whispered Eric, gazing around. 'I'm sure they are. It must be night-time. We must be . . . we must be *outside.*'

No sooner had he said it than they landed, softly, on a blanket of snow.

A huge full moon, five times the size of Earth's moon, blazed coldly in the sky. Rachel looked intently for signs of danger. Strange, twisted trees encircled them. Each tree was covered in thick snow, making the branches appear to bow in welcome. The snow was grey, not white. Rachel held out her hands in astonishment to catch the wispy flakes falling from the sky. They dissolved, smearing a dark wetness across her fingers. All around the same grey-coloured snow smothered the ground.

Eric said, 'Blimey. Where on earth are we?'

'You are not on Earth at all,' said a voice behind them.

The children jumped. Kneeling in the snow and smiling at them was the woman from the dream. She had luminous green eyes, spangled with purple and sapphire streaks. Straight black hair cascaded over her shoulders, and around her graceful neck she wore an elaborate diamond necklace shaped like a snake. The snake had two large ruby-red eyes, and Rachel saw them blink.

Next to her sat a hunched, squat creature who looked like an ancient dwarf.

'Who . . . who are you?' Rachel asked the woman.

'My name is Dragwena,' the Witch replied. She indicated the man. 'And this is Morpeth, my servant. Welcome to the world of Ithrea, Rachel.'

Rachel blinked. 'How do you know my name?'

'Oh, I know many things,' said Dragwena. 'For instance, Eric is afraid of me. Why do you think that is?'

Rachel felt Eric hiding behind her legs.

'I don't like this,' he whispered. 'Something's wrong. Don't trust her.'

Rachel shushed him, but also felt wary. Could this really be the same woman from the dream? She noticed that the dwarf-man shivered in his snow boots, while the bare-footed Dragwena seemed at ease, unaffected by the cold.

'We fell down a dark tunnel,' Rachel said. 'A creature with black claws—'

'It's gone,' said Dragwena. 'I scared it off.'

'But how could you have done?' Rachel protested. 'I mean, it was huge, and—'

'Forget the black claws,' said Dragwena. 'Put these on.'

Morpeth offered Rachel and Eric warm coats, gloves and scarves. Rachel studied the clothes, knowing they had not been in the dwarf's hands a moment earlier. The clothes fitted both children perfectly. Rachel placed a fur-lined scarf around her neck. As soon as it touched her skin she felt the scarf tuck *itself* warmly around her shoulders.

She shivered, wondering what might happen next. Was

this a magic world? Could she use the powers she had discovered between the worlds here? Who was this woman? She glanced at Eric nestled against her hip, and saw fear in his eyes.

'We need to get back home,' Rachel said firmly.

'Never mind that,' said Dragwena. She glanced at Eric. 'What are your favourite sweets?'

'I don't like sweets,' he said suspiciously.

Dragwena smiled. 'Really?'

'Well . . .' His expression became confused. 'Jelly beans, maybe.'

Rachel's mind lurched. She knew Eric *never* ate jelly beans.

'I thought so,' said Dragwena. 'Look in your pockets.'

'Wait a minute,' Rachel complained. 'We want to go home. We're not hungry. Oh!—'

A green jelly bean crept from a pocket in Eric's new coat. It crawled across his sleeve and leapt onto the ground. Another blue bean followed. Within moments they scrabbled from the coats of both children, wriggling across the snow, trying to escape.

Dragwena's eyes sparkled. 'Don't let them get away!'

Eric, without understanding why, immediately found himself racing after the beans, stuffing them into his mouth.

Morpeth, standing close, groaned inwardly. He saw that the jelly beans were really armoured spiders, rushing to find their way back to Dragwena's mouth. The Witch had done what he expected, placing a spell on the children for her own enjoyment – and to test Rachel.

Eric grew increasingly frenzied in his efforts to find and eat the jelly beans. A spider with four serrated teeth crawled inside his mouth. He chewed it ravenously while searching the snow for others that might have crept away.

Rachel was just as fascinated by the jelly beans as Eric. She held one close to her lips. It wriggled its little body, longing for her to bite into the juicy head, but the expression of disgust on Morpeth's face made Rachel hesitate. Even so, she had an aching desire to eat the sweet. Rachel kept looking at the unhappy Morpeth, and at the woman, shaking with laughter, and at the jelly bean, begging to be eaten. At last, with an enormous effort, she flicked the bean into the air. It landed on the woman's dress and rushed towards her lips.

Dragwena plucked the sweet from her chin and held it towards Rachel. 'Don't you want to eat one?' she asked. 'They're delicious.'

'No,' Rachel murmured uncertainly. 'I mean, yes, I'd like to eat them. I mean, I don't like jelly beans . . . I mean—' She looked at Eric, busy scoffing the beans near her feet. 'I mean—' She tried to think of anything except the sweets. 'What we want is to go back home.' Eric ignored her. 'That's right, isn't it? We want to go back home now.'

'Oh, shut up Rachel,' Eric said, juice dribbling from his mouth. 'Don't listen to her, Dragwena.' He stuck out his tongue. 'Rachel's talking rubbish, as usual.'

Rachel stared in disbelief at Eric. A few moments ago he had been frightened of the woman. What had happened to change his mind? She gazed nervously at Dragwena and the dwarf, sensing a huge threat. Should she try to escape? But that would mean leaving Eric behind . . .

The Witch slowly uncoiled from her kneeling position. She stretched her limbs like a cat, pushing out her arms and legs until she stood over seven feet tall. Pressing her toes into the snow she floated, a few inches above the ground, towards Rachel.

'Let's take a good look at you,' Dragwena said. She traced a complex pattern with her fingers on Rachel's nose and eyelids. 'Mm. You are an intriguing child. I see now you are what I was expecting. *More* than I expected. Answer a question: Eric came through the wall first. How did you both arrive together?'

Rachel was seized by caution, but felt compelled to answer truthfully. 'I just flew to him. It was easy.'

Dragwena laughed. 'What else did you do easily?'

Rachel told her everything that had happened between the worlds. She could not stop herself. Every minute detail of the journey poured out.

At last Dragwena seemed satisfied. 'What came to you so effortlessly, no child has ever done before, Rachel. None. And thousands arrived before you. Thousands of *useless* children. Follow me.'

Again Rachel could not stop herself. She reached forward to accept Dragwena's frozen outstretched hands. Deep in her mind Rachel's instinct told her to resist, stay close to Eric and get them both away. Instead, she found herself linking arms casually with Dragwena. Morpeth took Eric's small hand and all four together followed a path in the snow as if they had journeyed as friends along it many times before.

The black horses and carriage awaited. Inside, Eric sat next to Morpeth, no longer complaining, hands neatly folded on his knees. Morpeth stared blankly ahead. Rachel hardly noticed either of them. Instead, she inched closer to

Dragwena, completely fascinated by her looks and voice and gestures. Rachel forgot about wanting to get back home. She forgot about home altogether. She could not take her eyes off the Witch.

Dragwena caught a few flakes of snow falling through the open carriage window.

'Shall we fly?'

Rachel nodded eagerly.

The Witch whispered to the great black horses. Instantly, their hooves reared into the air, heading towards the Palace.

4

ARRIVAL
at the palace

Rachel remembered nothing about the long cold flight in the carriage. During the journey the Witch held her tightly, firing questions. Rachel told Dragwena all about herself, secrets even her best friends did not know. She spoke about her school, her parents, her favourite colours. She told the woman about everything she loved and hated. Dragwena seemed especially interested in what she hated.

When the Witch had discovered all she wished to know, the snake-necklace slithered from her throat. It entwined Rachel's neck, rocking her head gently backwards and forwards until she fell into a deep trance – a state from which only the Witch could awaken her.

As Rachel slumbered the Witch fought to contain her excitement. This girl-child was even stronger than she had expected. She had learnt how to fly between the worlds. She had resisted the sweets, even when specially urged to eat one.

I wonder, Dragwena thought, if this girl is the one I have waited so long for? She sighed. How many other girls had been so promising at first, only to prove too feeble to master the difficult spells of Witchcraft? Perhaps, after all, Rachel was just another weak child . . .

The Witch brought the carriage to the ground, opened the windows and called softly to her wolves. Within moments they loped alongside, nipping the forelegs of the horses, sharing her enjoyment of the evening.

Dragwena relaxed, dropping the pretty-woman face. Her ear stubs collapsed inside her skull. Her face flushed blood-red and her eyelids stretched sideways, meeting at the back of her head, mastering every detail of the world with perfect clarity.

On impulse, the Witch kicked the driver from his seat. She held the reins and thrashed the horses mercilessly for several miles, her four sets of teeth flashing in the light of the enormous moon of Armath.

Eventually, the Witch pulled the terrified horses to an abrupt halt at the bottom of the Palace steps. Several small people, who looked like Morpeth, waited.

'Hurry, you fools!' Dragwena snapped impatiently. 'Take them up!'

'B-but, my Queen,' stammered one. 'The chamber is not ready for guests.' He glanced sharply at two others. They wrapped Rachel and Eric, both sleeping, in warm blankets and shuffled up the Palace stairway.

'Not ready!' snarled Dragwena. 'Whose fault is this, Leifrim? Yours?'

He gazed down.

'No, it's my fault,' said another – a red-haired creature with the face of a girl and the wrinkled eyes of an old woman. 'Punish me!'

'Be quiet, Fenagel!' Leifrim hissed.

The Witch laughed. 'Perhaps I should punish you both. Father *and* daughter. The father for idiocy, and the daughter for speaking at all.' She lifted her throat towards the moon. Instantly, Leifrim shot into the dark sky, suspended several hundred feet above.

'What should I do to your father?' the Witch asked Fenagel. 'Does this deserve a severe punishment or only a small one?'

'Please don't hurt him,' Fenagel pleaded. 'He was only trying to protect me. It was me who forgot. I'll do anything you want.'

'Child,' said Dragwena, 'you have nothing I want. In my kingdom only I am allowed to forget, and I never forget *anything.*'

Leifrim was thrown hard against a nearby tree, his knees snapping as he hit the ground. For a few moments Dragwena enjoyed watching him struggle to untangle his smashed legs. Then she raised her arms and sprang from the icy ground, soaring toward the lights of the eye-tower.

As soon as the Witch was out of sight Fenagel ran to her father. He lay at the bottom of the tree, moaning loudly.

'Shush, Dad,' she said. 'It's all right. She's gone.'

Another man, with a short pointed beard, immediately took charge. He inspected Leifrim's injuries and ordered three others to take him to a small wooden hut, where they tended his cuts and made splints to support his broken legs.

Fenagel glanced angrily at the bearded man. 'Couldn't you have done something to help him, Trimak? You're supposed to be our leader! All you do is talk about how we must protect each other from the Witch. But you just stood by, like the others. How could you?'

Trimak bowed his head. 'A direct attack on Dragwena will never work,' he said. 'Your father understands that. If I had done anything to try to stop the Witch he knows she would have killed me.'

Leifrim nodded and Fenagel tearfully held her father's hands.

Leifrim whispered through his pain, 'We cannot harm the Witch, but perhaps someone else can. Morpeth managed to send a message using the eagle Ronnocoden, before they left the Gateway. He says this new child Rachel resisted Dragwena. She would not eat the sweets the Witch offered. Can you believe that! I was so excited by the news I forgot to check on preparations. Stupid – Dragwena never tolerates failure.'

Fenagel stared at his ruined legs. 'This is all my fault . . .'

'Don't blame yourself,' said her father. 'No one avoids Dragwena's punishments for long.'

Trimak stepped forward. 'Are you saying this girl Rachel resisted, and Dragwena let her live?'

'Yes,' said Leifrim excitedly. 'Apparently even the hag

Witch herself was impressed. Rachel must be special.' He turned to Fenagel. 'Remember the child-hope I told you about?'

'The one who will come from the other world?' Fenagel asked. 'The dark child who'll take us back to Earth.' She half-grinned. 'Wasn't that just a story?'

'Shush!' Trimak hissed. 'Exactly. It's just an old story. Watch over your father.'

Trimak issued instructions for preparing a stretcher and left the hut.

It was, as always, bitterly cold outside. A storm brewed over the entire northern sky. In the west a few lonely stars shone down. Trimak sighed, willing their twinkling light to hold off the storm. Southwards, the vast cold moon of Armath stared balefully down, its scarred surface offering no comfort. I wonder, Trimak thought, how many centuries that moon has looked down on our planet? Had it ever witnessed even one successful attack on the Witch? Never, he knew. Never.

He took a path near the Palace steps and tramped back to his own home. Muranta, his wife, heated some soup over an open fire as he told her about the evening's events.

She shivered. 'Do you think this Rachel could be the child-hope?'

'I doubt it,' Trimak said dismissively. 'We have seen so many girls come and go. They always seem promising, but Dragwena either destroys them or turns their strength to her own advantage.' He caught Muranta's eye and said menacingly, 'I sense the Witch has waited a long time for this girl to arrive. Perhaps Rachel will turn out to be another Witch. Think about that! In any case, I hardly dare to believe this Rachel will be able to help us.'

But secretly he wondered.

5

spells

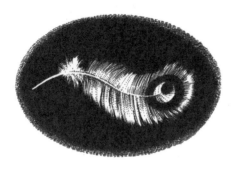

Rachel awoke late the next morning. She yawned loudly and dug her toes into luxuriously inviting sheets.

'Good morning, Rachel,' said a gruff voice.

She jumped up. 'Who's that?'

'Morpeth.'

Morpeth! Images crowded into Rachel's mind – the black claws in the cellar, meeting the snake-woman, and the dwarf. What had happened after this?

'Where am I?' Rachel demanded, trying to think clearly. 'Where is Eric? What have you done to him?'

'Your brother is safe,' said Morpeth. 'He's already had his breakfast and is playing nearby.' He pinched Rachel's toe. 'You, on the other hand, have overslept, sleepy-head.'

'Who is Eric playing with?' Rachel asked. 'Other children?'

'Of course! You are not the only children here. Our

world is full of children. He's playing hide-and-seek, I think.'

'In the snow?'

'Where better?' Morpeth laughed. 'Everything looks the same. Fantastic places to hide.'

Rachel stared at him. 'A world full of children? Why? Where do they all come from? Aren't there any . . . grown-ups?'

'I'll explain all that later,' Morpeth said. 'First let me welcome you again to the wonderful world of Ithrea.' He smiled brightly. 'You, our honoured visitor, are in Dragwena's Palace. Only special guests are given these rooms.'

Rachel studied the bed where she had slept. It was enormous, an ocean of scarlet sheets adorned with shimmering black serpents. Their ruby-red eyes all seemed to follow her.

'I'm not special,' said Rachel. 'I'm just like anyone else.' She examined the perfectly fitting pyjamas she wore. 'These aren't my pyjamas. Who—'

'A maid undressed you last night,' Morpeth told her.

'A maid?'

'You will have your own personal maid while you are with us. Her name is Fenagel.'

He looked across the room where a girl hovered awkwardly. Rachel saw she had the same strange bow-shaped wrinkles marring her eyes as Morpeth, making it impossible to tell her age. Neatly plaited red hair framed her thoughtful face.

Fenagel curtsied. 'At your service, miss.'

'I'm used to dressing myself,' said Rachel awkwardly.

'Dragwena says we should pamper you,' Morpeth told her. 'Fenagel will do anything you ask.'

'Anything you want!' gushed Fenagel. 'I'm not important, miss. I'm only a maid. Tell me what you need.'

Rachel did not know what to say. 'I don't . . . need anything. Don't call me miss. My name's Rachel.'

'Of course, miss – I mean, Rachel.'

'Time to get dressed,' Morpeth said. 'I'll wait for you in the Breakfast Room.'

'Do you know where my clothes are?' Rachel asked Fenagel, after he had gone.

'Oh Miss Rachel, you have lots to choose from. Come and have a look.'

Fenagel took Rachel into an area adjoining the bedroom. It was a wardrobe, but one so large that you could walk into the middle of it and still not see the walls at the other end. Everywhere Rachel looked, hanging on rails hundreds of feet long, there were clothes, thousands of them. And, as Rachel feasted her eyes, she found that all the garments turned towards *her*. Enticing dresses twisted to get her attention. A skirt flapped, showing ever-changing colours, rippling with pleasure as Fenagel gently stroked its hem. Several jumpers nudged aside blouses and lines of shoes clumped into view. At a warning glance from Fenagel each pair stopped at a respectful distance and permitted dainty socks and tights and leggings to dance between them. Finally all the clothes surrounded Rachel, forming a neat circle, silently awaiting her decision.

Rachel stepped back, gazing in wonder. One bold white

dress studded with glittering gems suddenly launched itself through the air, pressing against her chest.

'Get off me!' Rachel shouted, throwing it down.

'No. No. Try it on,' Fenagel laughed, wagging a finger at a blouse trying to creep over Rachel's foot. 'The dress won't hurt you!'

'But how can clothes—'

'Oh, I don't know!' said Fenagel. 'Dragwena makes it all happen. Are you going to wear that dress or not?'

'Am I . . . allowed to wear anything I like?'

'Oh yes, Miss Rachel. They're all for you.'

Overcoming her nervousness, Rachel quickly tried on several outfits, dashing between the racks of clothing and the many huge mirrors in the room. Each item of clothing fitted perfectly. She was too excited to care how. The original white dress studded with gems had crept to a corner of the rack, pining, looking forlorn.

'Shall I wear you?' Rachel asked it, expecting the dress to say 'Yes!'

'It can't talk, but it wants you to!' cried Fenagel. 'Isn't it gorgeous?'

Rachel was tempted. Instead, thinking she might need to go out into the snow, she picked a thick white pullover, some black trousers and a pair of sturdy grey flat shoes. She tiptoed from the wardrobe, wondering if the shoes would show her the way to the Breakfast Room. Instead, Fenagel took her, but would not go inside.

'Aren't you coming?' asked Rachel.

'I'm not allowed in,' said Fenagel. 'I mean, I've already eaten. I mean – I mean I'll see you later, miss!' She ran rapidly back down the corridor, as if she could not wait to get away from whatever lay behind the door of the Breakfast Room.

Rachel composed herself and gently rapped on the entrance.

'Come in, Rachel,' said Morpeth.

The Breakfast Room disappointed her. It was small, no bigger than her kitchen at home, containing only a plain round table set with two chairs. There were no eager spoons or tantalizing packets of cereal begging for her attention. Rachel sat down opposite Morpeth and attempted a smile.

'I'm hungry,' he said. 'Are you?'

'Mmm.' Rachel realized she had not eaten for ages. This instantly reminded her of Eric. 'Has Eric had breakfast? Where is he? He'll be scared if he doesn't know where I am.'

Morpeth laughed. 'I just checked on him. He's having a great time building a snowman outside. Hasn't mentioned you once! You can join him whenever you like. Let's have some food first, eh? What would you like?'

'Have you got any cereal?'

'Yep. Every kind of cereal you can think of, plus toast, eggs, all that stuff, and things you probably rarely have for breakfast – like gigantic, mouth-watering chocolate sandwiches.'

'Then I'll have chocolate sandwiches!'

'Well,' said Morpeth, relaxing in the chair, 'they're not here as such. You see, in our world you just imagine what breakfast you want.'

Rachel was suspicious, but recalled the wardrobe.

'For example,' he said, 'today I want some eggs, and I'll have sausages with them in the shape of, let's see – in the shape of *teapots.*'

The next instant a plate of steaming hot scrambled eggs and sausages appeared on the table. Each sausage looked exactly like a tiny teapot, with a spout, a handle and a fat belly.

Rachel's eyes widened as Morpeth picked one up. It had a little lid, like a real teapot. He popped it in his mouth.

'Delicious,' he said. 'You have a try.'

'I-I can't do that,' gasped Rachel. 'How did you do it?'

'Have you forgotten the magic you used between the worlds?' said Morpeth. 'This should be an easy trick for a clever girl like you.' He gobbled the eggs with a fork appearing in his hand. 'You see, this world is different from the one you come from. There's magic everywhere.'

'Everywhere?'

'Absolutely,' said Morpeth. 'And it's all waiting to be used. Magic can't wait to be used! A bit of practice is all you need. All you have to do is know what you want and make it appear.' He leaned towards Rachel. 'Close your lids,' he said, 'and see those nice chocolate sandwiches on a plate in front of you. It will work. I promise.'

Rachel shut her eyes and pictured the sandwiches. She saw them cut into little triangles, with lots of soft dark brown chocolate oozing out of the sides. But when she opened her eyes the table was empty.

'I bet you thought of the sandwiches,' said Morpeth, 'but didn't imagine them on the table in front of you. Am I right?'

Rachel nodded.

'Go on,' he urged. 'Try again.'

Rachel did and blinked in amazement as a pair of chocolate butties waited to be eaten.

Morpeth studied them. 'Promising, but you forgot something.'

She followed his gaze and saw that the bread was a fuzzy grey.

'Ugh,' she said. 'They look horrible.'

'They're not bad,' he grunted, biting into a fresh cream cake. 'You forgot to decide what *colour* you wanted the bread. Do you want it to be white or brown – or even silver? You see, the magic doesn't know what colour bread you want. Only you do. Have another go.'

Rachel made the bread white and fluffy. No butter, she decided. Just lots of chocolate. This time the bread was appealing.

'Don't be nervous,' said Morpeth, chewing on a big toffee-apple. 'Try one.'

Rachel gingerly picked up one of the sandwiches and took a small bite.

'Yeuch!' She threw it on the table. 'It tastes disgusting!'

Morpeth laughed out loud, big wrinkles creasing around his cheeks and mouth.

'It's not funny,' Rachel said.

'Ah, but you forgot something else!'

'Did I? No, I'm sure—'

'You forgot to imagine what the sandwiches would *taste* like!'

'Oh.' Rachel realized he was right. She quickly pictured the taste of mingled bread and chocolate and nibbled the edge. This time it was perfect.

Morpeth picked up the other sandwich. 'Can I have a munch?'

Rachel nodded, wondering how he could eat so much.

He took a great bite and chewed it slowly.

'Lip-smackingly gorgeous,' he sighed. 'I couldn't have done better myself. Try something else. How about some fruit?'

Rachel put an orange in the middle of the table. She frowned, wondering what was odd about it.

'Look closely,' Morpeth said. 'You know what's wrong. You don't need me to tell you.'

Rachel stared at the orange. It was round. It was the proper colour. She made the orange revolve slowly, while Morpeth sat back watching her in fascination. Suddenly she knew what was wrong: it didn't have the little dimples all oranges have. It was smooth, like an apple. A moment later she had made the dimples appear.

Morpeth snatched the orange from the table and tried unsuccessfully to peel it.

'Oh, I forget to make the skin real,' said Rachel, annoyed with herself.

'It doesn't matter,' said Morpeth. 'Tell me what you think of my next trick.'

An apple appeared, sitting on top of the orange. Rachel placed a banana above the apple. Morpeth added a peach. Rachel dumped a pineapple on the peach. They continued until the pile of fruit was impossibly high, nudging the ceiling.

Rachel shook her head. 'Why don't they fall over?'

'Because we don't want them to!'

Morpeth excitedly squeezed four more bananas into the

pile, and together they built impossible towers of fruit growing upwards and sideways. On impulse, Rachel scattered the piles and made all the fruit float around their heads. Morpeth hid the bananas behind the pineapples and Rachel hurled the melons into the wall, splatting juices all over the floor.

At last, she gazed at the mess. 'I suppose we've got to clean this up.'

'We could,' said Morpeth. 'Or we can imagine it cleaned up!'

Rachel did. In an instant the room was exactly the way it had been when she entered it.

'Can I change the room as well?' asked Rachel, not wishing to stop.

'Change what you like,' Morpeth urged. 'Change everything!'

Rachel took her time. She imagined the bare room was a huge dining hall. She created cutlery and suspended chandelier lights from the ceiling. On the table she conjured up hundreds of plates, heaped with roast chicken and potatoes and sweet corn and Yorkshire pudding.

What else? she wondered, trying to keep all the plates of food in her mind. She imagined the entire room made of glass filled with fish. What, *exactly*, should the fish look like? Goldfish tails or little puppy-dog tails? Ugly mouths or pretty ones? Rachel decided on slender rouge-lipped fish – with dainty green earrings hanging from their gills.

When she glanced up the room was transformed. She sat in a transparent glasshouse where teeming fish swam through the air. But it was still a disappointment. The earrings of the fish had turned yellow. Rachel made them green again. A second later they turned back to yellow – as if something else was influencing them. Rachel sighed, noticing that all the lights and plates of food she wanted were missing. She had focused so hard on the fish that she had forgotten to keep them in her mind.

'Oh dear, I'm no good, am I?' she said.

Morpeth looked exhausted, almost falling from his chair.

'Are you all right?' asked Rachel, anxiously.

'I'm fine, I'm fine,' he muttered. 'I'm just a little tired, child-hope.' He stared at Rachel, his expression a mixture of surprise and – fear?

'What does that mean?' Rachel asked. '*Child-hope.*'

'Nothing,' Morpeth said quickly. 'Nothing at all.'

Rachel gazed disconsolately at the Breakfast Room, seeing all the faults of her magic. Nothing was as she originally imagined it any longer. Even the fish were starting to look jaded and insubstantial now that she was not concentrating entirely on them.

'I'm rubbish at this,' she said.

Morpeth watched a fish swim around his knees. 'No. This room is . . . amazing. It's not perfect, but with practice you'll improve. You are incredibly gifted.'

Rachel blushed. 'Really?'

'Oh yes. Now, it's time to finish off your breakfast. I want to show you the gardens of the Palace, and later we'll pay Dragwena a visit.'

'The snake-woman I met yesterday?'

'Mm, but that's not a name she likes.'

'Sorry.' Rachel smiled hopefully. 'Can we play some more games first?'

'Later,' said Morpeth. 'First, I want to take my old bones

for a walk. Let's see how quickly you can finish your breakfast.' A plate of toast with several kinds of marmalade appeared next to Rachel. 'You do like marmalade, I hope.'

'Oh, I'm too excited to eat. I know – I'll imagine I'm full!'

Toast and marmalade filled her belly.

They both glanced at the empty plate and burst out laughing.

6

JOURNEY
in the sky

Morpeth led Rachel down a flight of stone steps leading from the Breakfast Room. He stopped at a huge round door made from burnished steel. It possessed no markings whatsoever, not even a handle or a lock.

'Is that the door to the garden?' Rachel asked.

'Yes.' Morpeth held his palm towards the metal surface and it silently opened.

Rachel watched him closely. 'You used magic, didn't you?'

Morpeth nodded.

'Why do you need a big door with a magic lock to go into the garden?'

'Dangers lurk outside,' said Morpeth. 'Remember the black claws? There are massive wolves too, yellow-eyed with teeth bigger than your face.' He grinned. 'You wouldn't want them to get in and bite you in half while you slept, would you?'

Rachel stepped back, suddenly frightened. 'I don't want to go out.'

'There's no need to be scared,' he reassured her. 'The wolves only come into the garden at night.'

Rachel peered cautiously out of the door. A shining blanket of light grey snow buried the grass. In the distance, surrounded by triangular-leaved trees, a frozen lake sparkled. She saw no yellow-eyed wolves. Could they be hiding behind the trees? What, she suddenly wondered, if just by *thinking* about it she could bring a wolf to life?

'I'll show you it's safe,' said Morpeth. He ran outside, cartwheeled in a big circle and shouted at the top of his gruff voice, 'Wolves, wolves, wherever you be, I've a big fat belly if you want to eat me!'

Rachel timidly took a step into the garden and then dashed to Morpeth, gripping him tightly.

'Come on,' he said. 'I'll race you to the lake!'

Rachel ran fast, but Morpeth's short thick legs were a blur of speed.

'You'll never catch me!' he bawled. 'I'm faster than the wind, I'm quicker than a cat, I'm so fast you'd never know I'm fat!'

He zigzagged across the garden, arms spread wide.

Rachel couldn't catch Morpeth, but she knew she could beat him. Remembering her journey between the worlds, she simply imagined herself landing near the lake. After a momentary whoosh of air she alighted comfortably by the shore. Morpeth staggered and almost fell over her.

'H-how did you do that?' he gasped, collapsing by a mushroom-shaped tree stump.

'It was easy. I just thought about it, like you showed me.'

Morpeth shook his head vigorously. 'No! I haven't shown you how to do that. I never taught you how to move from *one place to another*. Even I cannot . . . only Dragwena can do it!'

'It wasn't hard. I did it before.'

'But that was between the worlds! Dragwena places a special magic there to help all children brought to Ithrea. You did this yourself!' He stared at Rachel with a look of wonder on his face. 'You *are* the child-hope.'

'I am the what? You said that before, Morpeth. What do you mean? What is this child-hope?'

'I mean—' He checked himself, recovering his composure. 'I mean . . . you are the sneakiest little girl I've ever met! Fancy pulling *that* trick on me! Come on, let's go for a skate on Lake Ker.'

He leapt onto the ice, gliding on a pair of bright red skates. 'Whoopee!' Morpeth sang, turning perfect circles on one leg. 'Come and join me, Rachel. This is fantastic!'

She quickly imagined sparkling pink skates under her feet and they danced a joyful duet across the surface, as if they had been practising together for years.

Eventually they returned to the bank of Lake Ker for a rest. The Palace towered above them. Inside its high wall hundreds of thin black columns and battlements, with tiny, odd-shaped windows, pushed against the sky. Every contour was harsh, angular and threatening – the stone absorbing the daylight as if it hated it. One enormous slender tower in the middle of the Palace stood higher than all the others, like a giant needle piercing the sky. At its top was a large window, green in colour, and formed – Rachel tried to make out the shape. It looked like an eye. Where had she seen that shape before?

'Who built the Palace?' she asked. 'It looks old and it's so dark.'

Morpeth shuddered. 'It was built many years ago. That's all I know.'

But he knew far, far more than this. He knew Dragwena had built it thousands of years before, when she first arrived on Ithrea. He did not know why the Witch had come. She trusted no one with that secret. But he knew that Dragwena hated this world, and also hated all the children she had drawn from the Earth and enslaved – though she drew them always, seeking something she would never explain.

One night, many years before, Dragwena had brought Morpeth to the eye-tower of the Palace. She had taken great delight in explaining how each rock, each layer of the wall, had been dragged from the mountains by hand – by the small blistered hands of generations of children. It took centuries of labour. Most of the children died from hunger or cold as they carried its stones through the snow – or fell from the towers. It was a story that lasted many days and nights. With her perfect and ageless memory Dragwena recalled everything, the exact form of death for each child. She forced Morpeth to suffer also, understanding what she had done, and yet compelled to carry out her merciless commands nonetheless.

Morpeth sighed, and considered Eric. He was with the Witch now, being probed and tested. There was an unusual quality about the boy. A strength, a skill, though different from that of Rachel. Dragwena had instantly sensed it. If Eric's abilities were not interesting enough, Morpeth knew, Dragwena would soon find out and kill him. The boy might already be dead. What should he do about Rachel? How could he conceal her remarkable gifts from the Witch? Even now, from the eye-tower, he realized Dragwena was probably observing every movement he and Rachel made.

Rachel had been looking over the snow-covered Palace gardens and beyond. The only other buildings were a few simple huts around the Palace walls. Small, hunched figures like Morpeth moved slowly in and out. In the far distance huge jagged peaks jutted out of the ground.

'Are those mountains far away?' she asked excitedly.

'Ah, the Ragged Mountains!' said Morpeth, rousing himself. 'Why don't we find out? Let's fly there and take a look.'

Rachel giggled. 'Can we? We haven't got wings.'

'Oh, haven't we? Then we'll have to *imagine* them!'

Rachel expected wings to sprout from his arms. Instead, Morpeth simply peered into the distance.

'Today,' he said, 'I think I'll fly on the back of a giant sea eagle. Look – here she comes!'

Rachel followed Morpeth's gaze into the creamy winter sky. From far away, low across the horizon, a tiny point sped towards them. As she watched it grew larger, until first she saw its wings, then a pointed white head, and finally curved talons, each dwarfing Morpeth himself, sunk into the snow nearby.

Morpeth jumped nimbly on its back. 'Come on Rachel, let's go!'

His great bird leapt into the pallid sky.

'Don't leave me!' Rachel cried.

'You know what to do! Hurry, or I will beat you to the mountains!'

Rachel concentrated. What was the most superb bird? Another eagle? A dove? In her mind she formed the image of a great white snowy owl, yellow-billed, growing out of the snow. Even before the owl had fully taken shape she vaulted onto its back, gripping the neck feathers. Within seconds Rachel had soared hundreds of feet above the Palace, the cold wind scudding through her hair.

'I'll catch you! I'll catch you!'

The snowy owl, following her command, swiftly caught Morpeth's eagle. Perched side by side on their giant magical birds of prey they grinned at each other, stretching their necks to see what lay ahead.

'Let's fly over the Palace,' Rachel said.

'No! Straight to the mountains! A race!' Morpeth's eagle blazed high and away.

'You can't fly faster than me!' Rachel called out.

'Try to catch me! Use your magic!'

Within minutes they swooped amongst the mountain peaks, diving into the valleys and shooting over the high tops.

Rachel wanted to lead. She told her owl it was faster than any eagle, the swiftest creature that had ever taken flight – uncatchable – and streaked into the vast sky. Morpeth caught her effortlessly. Time and again Rachel strove to get away, but he always matched her speed.

'Why can't I stay ahead?' she complained over the wind.

'Because I can always imagine catching you up!'

'Then I'll imagine you can *never* catch me up!' Rachel whispered softly in the owl's ear and it sped into the distance.

'I just imagined,' Morpeth laughed, catching up again, 'that no matter how fast you flew I would *always* be able to catch up.' He drew alongside her. 'Can you imagine something I could *never* imagine? Can you, Rachel?'

She pondered this until Morpeth held out his arm to indicate the arc of the land glistening below.

'Look at that!' he marvelled. 'Look at the world of Ithrea!'

Rachel felt her heart race and drank in her surroundings. To the west and north of the Ragged Mountains piled even more peaks, halted by cliffs overlooking an endless sea.

'The Endellion Ocean!' Morpeth cried. 'An ocean of ice!'

Eastwards everything was unending grey snow, a monotony only broken by the towers of the Palace itself. In the south, a few black smudges that might have been forests huddled under the snow. Where were the children Morpeth said lived everywhere, Rachel wondered? Could there be towns hiding under the snow filled with them? Could she fly to where they lived? Could she – suddenly Rachel gasped and forgot altogether about children.

She had seen the storm-whirls.

There were eight of them, immense hurricanes, twisting in pairs in the corners of the world. Rachel flew higher, into the thinnest air, to peer inside. Nothing she had seen before could prepare her for the sheer size of these twisting towers of grinding wind. Black clouds belched from their tops, spreading horizontally out over the whole world of Ithrea, pumping snow like wrathful breaths in all directions. And inside each storm-whirl there was lightning too, not one flash, but endless streaks of lightning, setting the sky above ablaze like a gigantic camera flashlight.

Rachel breathed deeply, trying to take everything in. What kind of world was Ithrea? She suddenly longed for colour – any colour. There was none. The sky was dull white, the snow grey. Even the sun glowed feebly; it gave off virtually no heat and Rachel could look directly at its disc without hurting her eyes. A monochrome world, Rachel thought. A winter world. Like a black-and-white photograph. She looked at Morpeth and his blue eyes blazed in the whiteness of the sky.

'Does it always snow here?' she called across to him, suddenly shivering.

'Of course,' he replied. It is the will of Dragwena, he thought bitterly, though Rachel was not ready to hear the reason yet. 'Time to return to Lake Ker,' he said. 'We can't fly around all day.'

'Another race?'

'Why not? You haven't beaten me yet!'

He tickled the nape of the sea eagle and it plummeted towards Lake Ker. Rachel did not try to fly faster. She simply pictured herself already landing by the lake.

Instead, she found herself hovering beside the green eye-window of the highest tower of the Palace.

Looking out of the window, a few feet away, was Dragwena.

The Witch gazed at Rachel, stroking her snake-necklace. Rachel stared back uncertainly, sensing something was wrong.

'Come away!' Rachel ordered her owl, tugging its neck.

47

The bird refused to obey. Instead it moved even closer to the window, a few inches from the glass. The Witch smiled, pressed her lips against the window and blew Rachel – a *kiss*.

Immediately, a blast of wind struck the owl.

Rachel gripped the neck feathers, trying to steady herself. 'Take me away!' she ordered it. The owl slowly turned its massive head and opened its beak. 'No, don't!' Rachel screamed, seeing what it was about to do. The owl bent closer. It bit her hands – and nudged her off its back.

Rachel shrieked, clutching hopelessly for its tail feathers. And fell.

An icy wind tore through her hair. Glancing down, she saw another large tower yawning below, its needle point ready to impale her.

Rachel shut her eyes tightly, remembering how she had slowed her fall between the worlds. But the darkness between the worlds was an endless fall; this time she had only a few seconds to decide what to do. She had almost given in to panic when an idea abruptly struck her. It was an image – the image of a feather, a small white feather, drifting gently downwards. Rachel furiously held it in her mind, picturing how small she would be, how light, how calmly she would fall, rocking slowly back and forth in the wind.

At last she dared to look around. Huge snowflakes surrounded her, tossed by the wind, and she was being tossed with them. The whole sky blossomed with their greyness, crystal edges pressing hard, pouring dark freezing water over her body.

Suddenly, Rachel realized why the snowflakes were so

large – it was because *she* was so small: she had become a tiny feather. She could feel her new body drifting amongst the snowflakes, a prisoner of the winds. A moment later she landed comfortably on a ledge. A breeze picked her up and she wandered on the wind, strange sensations tingling across her new near-weightless body. She continued to drift to and fro, descending gradually with the huge snowflakes.

Then, through the blur of snow, she saw a figure racing towards her.

'Morpeth! Morpeth!' she cried.

He plucked the feather from the air, his giant fingers gripping her inside a dark world. Rachel waited in the quiet warmth of his hand, feeling safe. Moments later Morpeth placed her in the snow by Lake Ker and she watched him say three words from a great height.

Slowly at first, she felt her hands reappear. Arms grew from her shoulders, her lips flew past them – and a frozen Rachel staggered and shivered in the snow.

'Oh Morpeth,' she cried. 'What happened? The snake-woman stood there. She blew that kiss and—'

'I know. I know.' He wiped wet hair from her cheeks. 'You are safe now. I promise.'

Morpeth led her back to the Palace through the large steel door. Once again he opened it using magic. Rachel felt too distracted to notice. How could any of this be happening to her? The strange woman, Morpeth, the Breakfast Room, the owl, changing into a feather. How could any of it be real?

'Am I in a dream?' she asked. 'Am I going to wake up in a minute and have to go to school?'

'I wish you were,' he said. 'Or that this was *my* dream.'

'Morpeth, I want to find Eric and leave this place. I want to go home!'

Morpeth did not reply. Instead, he escorted her back to the Breakfast Room, where dry clothes waited. As Rachel dressed she noticed that the room appeared exactly the same as when she first entered it. The slender fish with earrings had vanished.

Morpeth sat her down. 'Rachel,' he said, his voice shaking slightly, 'I know you are frightened, but I need you to be brave.'

She nodded, not understanding, but trusting him.

'What you did,' he said, 'is change your form. You became something *different*.'

'A feather.'

'Yes, but it should not be possible. On this world only one has that power.'

'Dragwena,' said Rachel. 'I bet she can do it.'

'Yes.' He leaned forward and gripped Rachel's hands. 'In a moment I must bring you to the eye-tower. Dragwena will force you to undergo a severe test. I cannot warn you what it is, for that would betray me. It will not *seem* to be a test. It will come as a surprise and I will not be able to assist you. Do your best. I will try to protect you if I can.'

'I don't understand,' Rachel said. 'You saved me. I know you'll help.'

Tears splashed over Morpeth's sunken cheeks. He knew he had already told Rachel too much about what would happen in the eye-tower. He must seem *ruthless* when he brought the child to the Witch – Dragwena would be watching him closely when he arrived, and others would be observing his every move on the way.

'Morpeth, what's the matter?' Rachel asked. 'Don't cry. I'm all right now. I feel much better. Why are you so worried? What kind of test is it?' She felt Morpeth suddenly withdraw his hands. 'I don't want to take any test. I'm frightened.'

Morpeth sat with his head buried in his gnarled old fingers. He breathed deeply, and for a few moments his body became almost unnaturally still. When he looked at Rachel again his eyes had lost their friendly sparkle. He spoke in a different voice, much harsher than before.

'Dragwena is calling. We must hurry.'

'I won't see that woman,' Rachel said. 'She made the owl bite me. Where's Eric? I want to know what—'

'Shut up!' Morpeth shouted.

Rachel stepped back in shock. 'Morpeth, what's wrong?'

'Come on,' he growled, grasping her arm. 'Fun and games are over, girl-child. It's time to see how good you really are!'

7

RACHEL'S
TRIAL

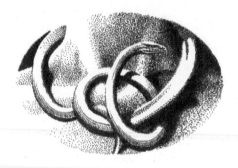

Morpeth trotted along several twisting dark passages, tightly holding Rachel's wrist, forcing her to run.

'Let go!' she protested, resisting him. 'I thought you were my friend.'

He laughed, dragging her up a vast flight of stone steps ascending the eye-tower. Rachel tried to understand what she had done wrong. Why was Morpeth behaving like this when he had promised to help her?

He eventually stopped outside a large arched door, flanked by two soldiers wearing short stabbing swords. In the middle of the door stood a snake-head handle, mouth open, as if ready to strike all visitors.

'I'm not going to see Dragwena,' Rachel told him. 'Not until I know Eric is safe.'

'Keep your mouth shut!'

'Don't tell me . . .' Rachel stepped back. 'I'm not doing anything else you say! Morpeth, why are you talking like this?'

He grinned. 'You'll soon find out.'

The door opened itself and Rachel peered inside the huge, dark chamber.

'You're on your own now,' said Morpeth. 'Keep your wits sharp or you won't come out alive.'

He shoved her inside and slammed the door.

Rachel, blinking in the semi-darkness, tried to get her bearings. She was drawn to the far end of the chamber, where a green window, shaped like an eye, gazed down on the Palace buildings. Dragwena stood beside the window, looking outward.

'Come in,' said the Witch, without turning round. Her voice was warm and inviting.

Rachel took a few steps towards Dragwena – and gasped. Eric's sleeping head poked from the blankets of a small bed.

'What have you done?' Rachel exploded, trying to shake Eric awake. He did not respond. 'If you've hurt him—'

Dragwena laughed softly.

'I want to go back home!' Rachel roared. 'Wake Eric up! Let us go!'

Dragwena turned, and Rachel saw a box in her hand. It was a plain black object, thin, that rattled. 'I have a present for you,' said the Witch.

'I don't want a present,' Rachel said stiffly. 'Tell me what you've done to Eric!'

Then she noticed a hissing sound coming from the box. Instantly, she had a sudden, almost painful desire to tear it open.

'What is it?' she asked, forgetting Eric. 'Oh, please let me have it!'

The Witch smiled and casually tossed the box in the air.

Rachel caught it, turning the box over and over, frantic to discover its contents.

'How do I get inside? I can't open it! I can't open it!'

'Isn't your magic powerful enough, child?'

Rachel held the box tightly, tearing at the lid, trying to picture a releasing clasp. There was something wonderful inside. She knew it would disappear if she didn't hurry. She gnawed the edges wildly.

Suddenly the lid ripped off. Rachel's grip had been so tight that the contents were spread over the floor. She looked down. In front of her was the board for a simple game she knew well: snakes and ladders.

What? she thought, intensely disappointed.

Then something happened that made Rachel change her mind – one of the snakes slithered to a new position. It twisted until it came to rest in the middle of the board. A second, much larger, snake uncurled until its head sat on the top row. All the other snakes, seven altogether, also jostled to find places. At last they were set, their tongues lazily tasting the air. Four ladders nestled between them. Three were tiny. One large ladder stretched from square three at the bottom diagonally right up to the top, two squares from the end.

'Do you like your present?' asked Dragwena.

Rachel smiled uncertainly.

The Witch knelt beside the board. 'Let's play a game. I like games.'

Two counters marched proudly from behind a chair, where they had come to rest after spilling from the box. A green counter span towards Dragwena. The blue counter jumped into Rachel's hand.

'You start,' Dragwena said.

Rachel nodded, fascinated, unable to take her eyes off the snakes. Her first throw of the game was a three. This placed her on the long ladder. She moved the counter up to sit on square ninety-eight.

'How fortunate,' said Dragwena. 'It will be hard to beat you if you play as well as that.' She took her own turn, threw a one and sighed. 'I'm rubbish at this,' she said, using the same words Rachel had spoken in the Breakfast Room, imitating her voice perfectly.

Rachel glanced warily at Dragwena. She knew this was no ordinary game. Could it be the test Morpeth had warned her about?

'What happens if I win?' she asked hesitantly.

'What would you like to happen?'

'To go home,' said Rachel. 'Both of us. That's all I want.'

'Throw a two or more,' said Dragwena. 'That is all you need. Then you can run back to Mummy and Daddy.'

'You *promise*.'

Dragwena imitated a different voice this time – Morpeth's. 'Of course! Don't you trust me, child?'

Rachel did not answer. Instead she picked up the dice, rubbing it against the soft part of her thumb. 'What happens if I lose?'

'That depends. It depends on how hungry the snakes are today. Continue to play. If you refuse I'll punish Eric.'

Rachel's heart leapt.

'Are you afraid?' Dragwena inquired gently, as if asking nothing at all.

'Of course I am! Why are you making me do this?'

'I have my own reasons,' said Dragwena. 'You are wasting time.' Her face transformed into Eric's. 'Don't let her hurt me,' Eric's voice pleaded.

Rachel considered trying to run for the door, then remembered the soldiers waiting outside.

'I won't need the soldiers if you have to be killed,' whispered Dragwena.

Rachel's hand trembled. She turned away from the Witch, no longer able to meet her gaze, pressing the dice hard against her palm.

I must throw a two! She concentrated furiously, as Morpeth had taught her, and released the dice. It clattered over the board.

Two neat dots faced up.

'I won! I won!' shouted Rachel.

'Nothing is as easy as that,' Dragwena said.

She touched Rachel's forehead. Instantly, she shrank to the size of a fingernail. Dragwena picked her up and placed her in the middle of the board.

'Now we'll see how strong you are,' said Dragwena. 'Watch out. The death-serpents are out to get you!'

One of the snakes immediately lurched towards Rachel, its head now twice the size of her body. Rachel ran across the board. Another snake turned towards her. She shrieked and jumped over its neck, dashing down the squares, towards the edge. Dragwena's own snake quickly uncoiled, spreading its thick body around the board like a wall, preventing any escape.

'What can I do?' screeched Rachel. 'It's not fair!'

'If you reach the final square you can still win the game. However, you might not like what's waiting for you.'

Rachel clearly saw what it was: the largest snake squatted on the final square. She would have to enter its mouth.

'Help me!' Rachel yelled, running up the board to escape a further snake zigzagging towards her.

'You have one chance,' said Dragwena. 'You need to use the ladders. Hurry, the snakes are restless!'

Rachel flew down the board to square three, hoping the ladder would take her up. It did nothing and the snakes continued to slide after her, chasing relentlessly. She stumbled and ran and jumped over their arched backs, but the snakes allowed her no respite. Finally, she no longer had the strength to evade them. The snakes closed in and trapped her in a corner. As they opened their jaws Dragwena, looking almost bored, sighed irritably.

Rachel stood facing the snakes. Terrified, she still tried to understand what Dragwena had meant about using the ladders. At last a sudden desperate idea struck her.

She gazed at the snakes and whispered '*Stop.*'

They halted, their forked tongues pressing against her body.

Rachel addressed them together: 'Eat the snake sitting on the last square.'

Instantly they obeyed. After a fierce struggle the largest

snake was smothered and killed. Only two snakes now remained alive on the board.

Rachel spoke to one of them. 'Move the ladder to square one hundred.'

The snake wriggled down the board, placed the ladder between its fangs, and positioned it on the final square.

Rachel calmly walked up the rungs of the ladder to the last square, put her arms by her side, and looked defiantly at Dragwena.

And the Witch looked back at her. *How* she stared at Rachel! She breathed raggedly, glancing at Rachel and the dead snakes.

Rachel did not wait for Dragwena to regain her composure.

'Attack her!' she instructed the two snakes still alive.

They leapt off the board, heading for Dragwena's throat, but the Witch's own snake quickly darted forward and swallowed them.

'H-how did you do this?' the Witch asked, dumfounded. 'You should not be able to defeat the snakes! No child has ever done it!' She leapt in the air. 'You *are* the one!' she gasped. 'After all this time . . .' She reached down to Rachel and touched her head, bringing her back to normal height. 'Oh Rachel, Rachel,' she cried, hugging her. 'Forgive me. I had to test you. You have no idea how long I have waited for you to arrive.'

Rachel pushed her away. 'Go away! Don't come near me!'

Dragwena turned triumphantly. 'You hate me now. But soon you will learn to adore everything that I am. We will rule together on Ithrea, and on *your* world too.'

'You promised to let us go if I won. You *promised!*'

'I lied,' said Dragwena. 'I have never kept a promise to a child, and I never will.'

Rachel kicked the Witch hard.

Dragwena jumped back in surprise. Four sets of teeth momentarily appeared on her face, snapping at Rachel. As soon as Dragwena knew Rachel had seen the teeth she dropped the pretty-lady face entirely. The tattooed eyes which stared at Rachel were expressionless.

'You should not enrage me,' Dragwena warned her. 'I could destroy you in a second.'

Rachel backed away, appalled by the Witch's true appearance. 'What do you want with me and Eric? What *are* you?'

'A Witch,' Dragwena whispered. 'And soon you will also be one, Rachel. A very powerful Witch.'

'What? No, I won't,' Rachel said. 'You're . . . how dare you keep us here, playing these games? I don't care what it's all for. I *won't* help you.'

'Child,' replied Dragwena, 'do you think you have any choice in the matter? From now on you will always be at my side.'

Rachel felt sick with hatred. 'Let me leave!'

'In a moment,' said Dragwena. 'You are tired. First you should have a rest. After that – we'll see.'

Rachel inexplicably yawned. For some reason she did feel tired. She fought it, knowing the Witch was responsible.

'Your lids are drooping,' said the Witch. 'You can hardly keep them open.'

Rachel's eye-lids fluttered and closed. With a huge effort she managed to open them.

'I'm not tired at all,' she said, yawning again. 'I'm wide awake. I don't want to sleep. I *won't* sleep.'

'Get into the bed with Eric,' the Witch said. 'I know you want to.'

Rachel found herself crawling under the sheets, pulling the quilt around her. 'I'm not tired,' she said weakly. 'I won't do what you ask.'

'Have a long rest,' said the Witch. She tucked the quilt around Rachel's shoulders and kissed her on the cheek. 'I promise you will have lovely dreams.'

Rachel's face nestled into the pillow. 'I'm not tired . . . not . . . tired.'

In a few moments she was asleep.

While Rachel slept Dragwena reached into her mind and created a *dream-sleep*, the transforming spell needed to begin changing Rachel from child to Witch. Dragwena had never used such a powerful spell before on Ithrea. Would it work on Rachel? Countless children had come and gone, some gifted like Morpeth, but none had the magical intensity that Rachel displayed. Could she control Rachel? Already she felt Rachel's power swelling. If she acted quickly she could mould Rachel into anything she needed. Trembling with excitement, Dragwena planted the layers. Slowly, carefully, she chose memories from her past, hatreds and fears and longings, events and feelings that would overpower Rachel's mind, condition her, prepare her for a new destiny.

Once the dream-sleep was ready, Dragwena turned to Eric. She sensed a power within him she had never faced before, yet her testing earlier in the day had revealed no magic in the boy – surprising given Rachel's extra-ordinary power. Still, he was young and did not have Rachel's defiance. His personality should be easy to break and reshape. She touched Eric's temple, probing into the cortex, searching for the control roots of his brain.

Instantly, the Witch was thrown across the chamber.

She screamed, every muscle in her hand clenching in spasm.

An attack!

Dragwena lay on the floor, pondering, waiting to re-cover. What could it mean? After a few minutes she activated her own mental defences, returned to the bedside and delicately probed Eric's thoughts.

She sensed several layers of protection in Eric's mind and was bewildered – no human had this gift. This was no ordinary child. She should have realized that and been more careful. Dragwena sat for over an hour, observing Eric closely, knowing he was asleep, that the child had not deliberately thrust out. When she felt ready she once again delved tentatively within his mind, searching his memories for a clue. Nothing – only a child's simple joys and frustrations. Eric, she realized, was not even aware of his abilities. Could they have been planted? By whom? Dragwena sat back in frustration, wanting to study further. Eric's tantalizing gift must wait, she thought. I will strip his mind of the secret later. For now Rachel's power is all I need.

Carefully, avoiding Eric's defences, Dragwena planted a spell in the outer layer of his brain. It had been a long time since she had used this particular spell – so weak that it was almost undetectable, so simple that it would be hard to block even if detected.

The spell was perfect for what she needed.

8

the council of sarren

The Witch finished her work on Eric, left the eye-tower and met with Morpeth.

'You have instructed Rachel well,' she announced. 'Her abilities are great.'

Morpeth bowed. 'I did nothing. The child took control from the start.'

'That is obvious,' said the Witch. 'Her magic is beyond all except my reach. Take Rachel back to the east wing tonight and prepare a room with her wardrobe closer to my chamber. In the morning bring her to me. You will have no further part in her training.'

Morpeth nodded. 'Did you test her with the box?'

'Yes. And she conquered it! She defied it!'

'That has never been done!' marvelled Morpeth.

'Indeed. She will do many things no child has done before.' Dragwena glanced warily around the corridor. 'I have placed Rachel in a sleep that will start her transformation into a Witch. Tonight I want you to stay with her, Morpeth. Guard her personally. Do not allow her to be awakened until she is ready. Also, ensure Eric stays in her room tonight. He has no magic, but may prove valuable nonetheless.'

'As you wish. Will Rachel remember anything when she wakes?'

'Nothing important,' said Dragwena. 'Her past will vanish when the dream-sleep is over. She will remember nothing about her family, even Eric. Instead, her mind will be prepared for the final training she needs. I will undertake this myself.'

'What should we do with Eric?'

'Kill him,' said the Witch. 'Not yet, though. He may still be useful. I will tell you when.'

Morpeth bowed again and the Witch returned to the eye-tower. Morpeth arranged for two maids to carry the sleeping children back to the east wing and gave them Dragwena's orders.

Once he was alone again with Rachel and Eric, Morpeth buried his face between his knees. He sat for a long time, thinking about what should be done.

I must act tonight to save Rachel, he realized. Tomorrow will be too late.

Masking his face he left the Palace, treading cautiously across the snow towards the house of Trimak.

Muranta woke first. 'Wake up, Trimak, you old booby,' she

said, digging her arm into his ribs. 'There's someone banging on the door.'

'Well,' Trimak muttered sleepily, 'they can't be enemies making that racket.'

He put on a pair of old slippers and padded along the corridor.

Muranta lit a candle. 'Who can it be at this hour?'

Trimak listened to the heavy knocking, counting each rap. Four fast knocks, one slow, three more fast raps – Morpeth, and he was in danger!

'What's up?' Trimak asked, quickly shutting the door behind him.

'It's the girl, Rachel,' said Morpeth. 'She survived the box.'

'What! Did you see it happen?'

'Of course not! Dragwena does not allow me in the chamber at such times. But she could not contain her excitement. She intends to turn the child into another Witch.'

'Let's be careful before we act,' Trimak said, struggling to remain calm. 'This could be a trick. It would not be the first time the Witch has questioned your loyalty.'

'No, I'm sure this is not one of Dragwena's games,' said Morpeth. 'I tested Rachel earlier. She changed into a feather and shape-shifted from the Palace to the shore of Lake Ker. She did both effortlessly.'

'Then she *is* the child-hope,' Muranta whispered.

'Did Dragwena see everything you saw?' Trimak asked.

'She must have done,' groaned Morpeth. 'You know how closely the Witch observes during the trial period, especially gifted children. Once I realized Rachel's strength I tried to lead her to the mountains, but Dragwena drew her to the eye-tower.'

'You let her fly near the tower!' thundered Trimak. 'How could you let the Witch get so close?'

Morpeth lowered his face.

'Never mind,' sighed Trimak. 'I suppose if Rachel survived the box Dragwena knows everything anyway. Where is Rachel now?'

'In the east wing,' said Morpeth. 'Tomorrow morning Dragwena is moving her to the eye-tower.'

'Then we must act tonight, before it's too late.'

Morpeth nodded.

'I will call the Council of Sarren,' said Trimak. 'We will decide together what must be done.'

It was late in the kingdom of Ithrea. Steady snow fell across the whole night world, refreshing what little had melted during the day. Most of the slaves of the Witch – the *Neutrana* – were already asleep, enduring the troubled dreams of Dragwena, awaiting her commands. Amongst the Neutrana lived a few who had managed to free themselves from the Witch's control. They called themselves the *Sarren*, after a man now long dead who supposedly was the first to refuse to obey the Witch. Morpeth was one of the Sarren, as were Trimak and his wife Muranta, Fenagel, her father Leifrim and several others. They met rarely, communicating through special signs, obeying Dragwena's endless duties, while keeping watch – keeping watch on all the new children who arrived and, where they could, trying to help them.

Trimak sent the alert by personal messenger – extremely

dangerous, but the circumstances demanded it. Gradually over the next hours stealthy, coded taps on window and door awakened Sarren close to the Palace. They knew the danger call and slipped quietly from their beds. Each headed for Worraft, the guarded secret cave deep under the foundations of the Palace.

Within an hour over thirty of the Sarren had arrived.

Trimak glanced around, counting as shadowy presences hurried to find places on the stone seats along the walls of the great cave. He noticed Fenagel struggle in with Leifrim, pushing him along on a kind of wheelchair-stretcher.

'It's time to close the door,' said Trimak. 'We can wait no longer.'

Morpeth traced a circle on his forehead, and a wall of rock came down from the ceiling of the cave, blocking the entrance. No one could now enter the cave or leave it. The meeting could begin.

The gathered Sarren murmured nervously. They were concerned and with reason: no such conference had been called for many years. Trimak clapped his hands and silence descended.

'Why have you called us so recklessly, without warning, Trimak?' demanded a voice from the dark.

'In haste there is danger,' Trimak agreed. 'The reasons will soon be clear enough. Let Morpeth speak.'

Morpeth arose from his chair and addressed the assembly. 'I have important news,' he announced. 'I believe we have found the child-hope!'

Uproar broke out in the cave. Morpeth told them everything he had seen and Dragwena's plans for Rachel.

'Even if this is the child-hope,' someone called out, 'what can we do? Dragwena already has command of the girl. We are surely powerless to assist her.'

'We have a slim chance,' said Morpeth. 'Rachel has been left in a chamber I can reach. We can sneak back to the Palace and kidnap her.'

'Too dangerous,' snarled the same voice. 'Her spies will see us coming.'

'If many attempted the kidnap that would be true,' said Morpeth. 'But Dragwena trusts me. I can get safely back into the Palace without anyone noticing. If I'm seen I will say I am on the Witch's business. Everyone knows who I am. No one will dare to question me.'

Another voice said, 'What if this girl refuses to help us?'

Trimak stepped forward. 'I have considered this possibility.' He looked out boldly at the Sarren. 'If Rachel refuses to help us – then we will be forced to kill her *ourselves.*'

An awful silence fell on the cave.

'Trimak! Remember our pledge!' bellowed another Sarren. 'The shedding of child blood is the dark work of the Witch and her Neutrana slaves. I, for one, could not do this. How can you even suggest it?'

Several voices muttered their agreement.

Trimak sighed and held up his hand. 'I understand your fear,' he said. 'Do you think I have come to such a conclusion easily? Think: if Rachel will not assist us she is too dangerous to leave alive. We may hide the girl here for a while, but in time Dragwena will surely find and transform her. There will be no escape for us if this happens. With their strength combined they will quickly find and slaughter all Sarren.'

'And will you kill Rachel yourself, Trimak?' someone asked. 'Would *you* be prepared to do it?'

'I will do it if it must be done.'

'It should not come to that,' Morpeth said. 'If the child survived the box she has an innate strength Dragwena will not easily conquer; and remember, the Witch has had little time to work on Rachel's mind. If we act at once I am certain we can persuade her.'

Fenagel spoke up. 'Dragwena is so powerful. Is Rachel strong enough to fight the Witch? She seemed just like an ordinary, friendly girl when I was with her today. Even the simple magic of the Palace dresses came as a surprise. Imagine what Dragwena could throw at her! I think you're expecting too much, Trimak.'

'It's hard to argue against what you say,' said Trimak. 'But consider: for hundreds of years we have spoken about the legend of the child-hope, the girl who will defeat the Witch and free us all. I know at times we have all felt foolish, clinging onto this idea.'

Within the cave most heads nodded.

'But if we are to have any chance of defeating the Witch,' continued Trimak, 'then aid *must* come from the world outside. We all know this. Morpeth is our best weapon, but even combined with all our magic he's not strong enough to confront Dragwena. I can't promise any of you the child-hope is real. However, from what Morpeth tells us Rachel possesses magical powers far greater than any we have witnessed before. She *may* be the child-hope. No one among us has ever mastered skills she has developed in a single morning of play.'

He paused, to ensure that his next words were understood by everyone. 'Let me warn you all: if we do not try to use this girl's power to help us you can be sure Dragwena will not hesitate. She will take Rachel and turn her into an enemy whose ferociousness we can hardly imagine.'

He gazed at the faces in the darkness. 'Remember we speak now for all Sarren, many of whom cannot be here. To waver in our decision would deliver them all to Dragwena. I believe we have no choice. We must grasp the girl tonight, while we have a chance. If we wait even a few hours it will be too late.'

He peered around the cave. 'Are there any more questions? Does anyone have a different view?'

The cave was silent. Trimak waited several patient seconds before closing the discussion – the decision so grave everyone must have a chance to speak.

'In that case,' he said, 'I take it we are agreed. Morpeth will kidnap Rachel from the Palace tonight and bring her to Worraft. Now I ask you to return quickly and quietly to your homes. It will be noticed if you are away for too long.'

Morpeth again used his magic to open the door of the cave and the Sarren left rapidly, whispering to each other.

Once they were alone, Trimak noticed Morpeth deep in thought.

'What is it, my friend?' he asked. 'You have a trial ahead of you. Are you worried Dragwena may be lying in wait?'

Morpeth shook his head. 'I am not concerned for myself,' he said. 'Something you mentioned earlier has been gnawing at me. I wonder whether Dragwena does suspect I'm a rebel. She's certainly bored with me. It's obvious she wants a new, younger slave to replace her old guide.' He rubbed his chin. 'Perhaps, after all, this Rachel is not the girl she appears to be, merely one of the Witch's spies. Dragwena can make a creature look and behave as she wishes. Perhaps she transformed a Neutrana into the shape of a girl and gave her some extra powers just to tempt me.'

'Didn't you see Rachel arrive from Earth?'

'What I *saw* means nothing. Dragwena could have set me up. My heart tells me to trust Rachel, but Dragwena could easily have deceived me.'

Trimak bowed his head thoughtfully.

'There is more,' said Morpeth. 'Rachel has a brother who came with her through the Gateway. I must try to rescue Eric, too. Dragwena is bound to kill him if Rachel escapes.'

'Too dangerous,' replied Trimak. 'You must only worry about yourself and Rachel.'

Morpeth shook his head. 'We already ask so much of Rachel. Do you think she will forgive us if we do not try to save her brother?'

Trimak paced the cave, his expression anguished. 'Your safety and that of Rachel are too important to risk. I hate to be so merciless, Morpeth, but forget the boy. We have waited hundreds of years for this moment. We will lie to Rachel about Eric if we must.'

'That may not work,' said Morpeth. 'I have already sensed how quickly Rachel's magic is developing. If we lie, and she discovers this, she will never trust us. Never.'

Grudgingly, Trimak said, 'Oh . . . very well. But surely someone else can plan Eric's rescue?'

'No. Only I know the commands to lead them both safely from the Palace.'

'How will you bring them here?'

Morpeth grinned ruefully. 'A boy and girl over each of

my handsome shoulders, I should think. Dragged here on my tired old legs. I daren't use my magic so close to Dragwena. She knows my pattern too well.' He met Trimak's solemn gaze. 'Time to leave, I think. If Dragwena is preparing a welcome at the Palace, it would be rude to keep her waiting!'

He hugged Trimak and rapidly strode out of the cave.

Trimak now stood alone in the deep silence of Worraft. He thought about the work ahead for Morpeth and shuddered with fear. Have I sent my best friend to his death? he wondered. Could Rachel be a spy, or already under Dragwena's sway?

He knelt on the cold floor and, while he waited, felt the pressure of a small knife against his hip. He unsheathed it and deliberately held the blade towards the light, forcing himself to look at the sharp edge – to consider what might have to be done.

9

the child
army

While the Council of Sarren debated Rachel slept. Her
body lay slumped in the east wing of the Palace where
Morpeth had left her, breathing slowly and peacefully at
first. Then her pulse quickened as the dream-sleep of the
Witch gradually took hold. The dream would spare her
nothing – only by feeling Dragwena's own desires and
hatreds could she be transformed into a Witch.

Within the dream-sleep Rachel experienced the past life
of the Witch.

Rachel saw things she would rather never have seen. She
saw lakes and streams; when Dragwena touched them they
turned to ice. She saw a snake, slithering from Dragwena's
neck in a silent attack. She saw a boy no older than Eric
being hunted by a pack of wolves. She witnessed children of

Ithrea long dead whom the Witch had killed. Dragwena forced Rachel to gaze into their faces and know their names. For a moment, Rachel even saw Morpeth as a young boy newly arrived on Ithrea – a boy with sandy-coloured hair and big blue eyes. 'Ready?' he asked. He opened his clenched hands and a tiny bright bird, no larger than a penny, flew into the air. 'I did it!' he gasped. Dragwena stood there, gazing fondly. 'You are my favourite child, Morpeth,' she said.

This memory, like all the others, lasted only a moment. Rachel could do nothing to stop them or shut them out. They streaked by as Dragwena selected all the memories of her past she needed Rachel to know, forcing her to watch, faster and faster, until each image became a blur of pain.

At last the memories stopped and Rachel, still in the dream-sleep, stood side by side with Dragwena herself in the eye-tower. The Witch's skin oozed its blood-red brightness, and Rachel watched spiders crawling beneath her teeth.

'Do I frighten you?' Dragwena asked softly.

'Yes,' said Rachel. 'You want me to be frightened. Why have you shown me all this? The things you have done . . . make me hate you even more than before. I'll fight you if I can.'

'You don't understand yet,' whispered Dragwena. 'I do not wish to fight. I already know that if I threaten Eric you will do anything I ask.'

'Yes,' said Rachel. 'I've seen what you do to children.'

'Children mean nothing. When you have as much power as I their lives are meaningless. You will soon have that power and feel the same.'

'I'll never feel that way. I don't want your power, Witch!'

'I would like to show you one more thing,' said Dragwena. 'It contains my most terrible memory, one that shames me. Do you want to see it? If you can resist my worst memory I will know that I can never use you. Then you will be free.'

'No. You'll kill me and Eric. I know you will.'

'This memory holds a secret I have shown no one else,' Dragwena said. 'It will also show me at my weakest. That could be useful if you need to fight me. Perhaps you can save yourself and Eric after all. Surely you want that chance?'

'Show me, then!' Rachel shouted.

Instantly, Rachel found herself thrust back in time. She gasped, realizing that she was no longer on Ithrea. She stood outside an enormous cave. The cave was surrounded by thousands of savage-looking children, each carrying swords and knives. Their faces were sweaty and ferocious.

'Where am I?' asked Rachel. 'Who . . . are these children? What have you done to them?'

'We are back on your Earth, in an age forgotten thousands of years before your birth,' Dragwena's distant voice answered. 'See how the children loved me then.'

Earth!

Rachel watched the Child Army standing with swords erect, chanting the Witch's name: 'Dragwena! Dragwena! *Dragwena*!' they cried with one great voice, adoring her. As the children called out Rachel saw Dragwena appear from a cloud. She swooped like a swallow over the army's raised swords, tenderly brushing the sharpened tips.

'What was this army for?' Rachel asked, trying to remain calm.

'I fought a battle against three Wizards on your planet,' Dragwena said. 'Always we have waged this war, Wizard and Witch, across many worlds and across all time. I had no interest in the children, but I knew the Wizards would come to protect the most fragile creatures on your world. They always do. But I had many years to prepare each child before they arrived, and when the Wizards came at last I surrounded myself at all times with my loyal Child Army. The Wizards did not dare attack me directly – they were afraid of injuring the children. That was their weakness, and I used it. I sent the children themselves to slaughter the Wizards. They hid underground. My children followed. I raised an army of a million, taught them my ways, and sent them deep inside the world with shields and swords of magic to seek out the Wizards and kill them.'

Rachel saw the shining look on each child's face as it held a sword aloft.

'They worshipped me,' said Dragwena. 'Each child would have killed with its bare hands if I ordered it. Their minds were full of hate. They hated the Wizards as I hated. They killed as I killed: without hesitation, without guilt.'

Rachel shivered, but also felt defiant. 'Do you think by showing me this I will do what you ask?' she scoffed. 'These children are twisted. Everything about you disgusts me!'

'Watch the final battle with the Wizards through my eyes,' said Dragwena. 'I have trapped them within the deepest cave in the world, and I go now to destroy them.'

Rachel felt herself inside Dragwena's body. She soared

into the cave mouth. Inside, all three Wizards squatted in tattered clothing. One Wizard stood up shakily when the Witch entered.

'Get on your knees, Larpskendya, leader of three,' Dragwena snarled. 'Kneel and beg. Or I will make the pain of your death last longer than this entire war.'

Larpskendya gazed calmly at her. 'You cannot harm us,' he said. 'Put down your weapons. You have already lost.'

'Lost?' Dragwena answered scornfully. 'How pathetic you are! This is where your great magic has left you – hiding in your rags! Will *you* stop me, Larpskendya? Will you take my sword and strike me down?'

'Not I, you fool,' he said.

Larpskendya turned to his companion Wizards and they all laughed at Dragwena.

Instantly, she uttered a spell of evil over her sword and thrust it into Larpskendya's heart. As it pierced his flesh a radiant blue light flashed from the wound. The light sprang from the cave and poured into the hearts of all the children waiting outside. Each child felt Dragwena's sword enter its own chest and howled in agony.

Dragwena stared in shock at the Wizards.

Lazily, Larpskendya plucked the sword out of his chest. The wound vanished. He met her disbelieving look, his eyes sparkling with many-coloured light. Then he touched his tattered robe.

Dragwena was brought to her knees, barely able to lift her face.

'You do not understand, do you?' Larpskendya said. 'Even *now* you do not understand.' He shook his head sadly. 'Your desire to kill us is so strong that you have forgotten the laws of magic.'

Dragwena stared. His words meant nothing to her.

'For every spell of evil there is a spell of goodness that will prevent it,' he explained. 'How could you have forgotten that simple law? You have been trapped, Dragwena. When you struck me with your sword we made every child in your army feel its pain and understand the evil enslaving them. They are coming now. They are coming for *your* blood, not ours. As you said yourself, they hate with your hate. They will show you no mercy.'

Dragwena listened, hearing the sound of thousands of children's feet running into the caves. As they came they scraped their knives against the stone walls, sharpening them. The sound was unbearable.

Dragwena tried to build a protective barrier at the mouth of the cave, but the spell merely burned uselessly in her mind. Her powers, she realized, were gone. The children continued to rush towards them, their cries deafening.

'Your magic has been stripped away,' said Larpskendya. 'You will never be allowed to rule over humankind again.' He stared coldly at her. 'What does it feel like to be as powerless as those you once enslaved?'

Dragwena said nothing.

'There are many forms of death we could have chosen for you,' Larpskendya said. 'Perhaps we should kill you, as I know you will never change your ways, Dragwena. But all life, even your life, has some meaning. Therefore, we offer another choice. I have created a young planet for you: Ithrea. There you will be banished for the remainder of your days. Many of your powers will be returned, those to help shape the new home to your needs. But there are no creatures such as these children to bend to your will, merely plants and a few simple animals.'

Dragwena considered the Ool World, the distant planet of Witches from which she came. Surely the Sisterhood would find her in time, wherever she was sent. They would always search for her, and if she was killed they would revenge her death.

'The Ool Witches will never find you,' said Larpskendya. 'The world of Ithrea is obscured from their leering view. You will be alone. Always.'

Dragwena spat at his feet. 'You had better kill me now, Wizard. I'll find a way back to this world.'

'Do you think I will leave this planet unprotected?' said Larpskendya. 'I will give the children of Earth new gifts to use against you if they should ever be needed.'

Dragwena laughed. 'Even you cannot create a child with the power to threaten me! I have worked on them for generations. They are weak. They can be made to obey, but have no flair for real magic. A million breedings could not make a human child with enough strength to concern a Witch.'

'We shall see,' said Larpskendya. 'In any case, know this, Dragwena: my song will always be on Ithrea. If I am called, I will return.'

The Witch cursed him. 'Get on with the banishment – before I tear out the hearts of the first children who reach us.'

The Wizards immediately held hands.

The next moment Dragwena stood alone on a new world. She looked about her. The skies were blue and the sun shone radiantly. Shimmering lakes sparkled in the sunshine and birds twittered amongst branches and leaves bursting with vitality.

Dragwena dragged her hands across her face. The loveliness of this world only enraged her. The destruction of the Wizards she had worked for, strived so long for, had been snatched away. Her hatred of them and the children who had turned against her returned, and she let out a scream of anguish.

I will return, Dragwena pledged. I will return and kill you all!

Rachel was lost inside the overwhelming hatred of the Witch. She fought to keep control, to remember who she was, but the Witch thrust further and further into Rachel's mind until she could no longer resist. At last, deep within the dream-sleep Rachel, too, swore to return and kill the Wizards and the children. As the Witch hated, so Rachel hated.

Lying in her soft bed in the Palace Rachel clenched her fists and dreamt of revenge.

10

awakeninG

Morpeth burst into Worraft, a sleeping Rachel and Eric under each arm.

'Far too simple,' he said, placing them on the cave floor. 'Something's wrong.'

'You rescued both!' marvelled Trimak.

'Yes, but it was too easy to escape the Palace. There were few Neutrana, and the east door stood unprotected. You know Dragwena always stations two guards there.'

'Were you followed?'

'I saw no one, but Dragwena has a thousand eyes.'

'Our scouts are close to the Palace and the cave,' said Trimak. 'They should be able to give us some warning if we're in any danger.' He looked with concern at Rachel. 'I see the child-hope still sleeps.'

'It's a dream-sleep planted by the Witch,' said Morpeth. 'She may not awaken for several hours.'

'What about Eric? Has the Witch been working on the boy, too?'

'Possibly,' said Morpeth. 'There is something strange about Eric.' He turned slowly towards Trimak. 'In fact, I know *exactly* what is unusual about him. I sense no magic, none. There is always a trace, even in the least gifted children.'

'Yes,' mused Trimak. 'Eric is different. Perhaps that is why Dragwena is interested in him.' He looked at Rachel. 'What kind of dreams would Dragwena give the girl?'

Morpeth grunted. 'Nightmares, without doubt.'

'Wake them up,' said Trimak.

'We can't! I've no idea what will happen if Rachel is woken too soon. We must let her wake when she's ready.'

'No,' Trimak said firmly. 'I understand your concern, but you said yourself that Dragwena's spell is intended to turn Rachel into a Witch. Even now the dream-sleep is probably conditioning the girl. We can't give the Witch any advantage.'

'It could kill Rachel,' said Morpeth. 'I've no idea how powerful this spell is. It is wrong to—'

'Do it!'

Reluctantly, Morpeth placed two bent fingers against Rachel's forehead. She moved, but remained asleep.

'Use *full* force,' Trimak demanded angrily.

'I daren't! If Rachel is the child-hope we can't risk her safety.'

'I can't risk the safety of the Sarren, either. Try Eric first. Perhaps the Witch also put him in a dream-sleep.'

This time Morpeth placed both hands against Eric's temple. He shot up, blinking in fright. Morpeth and Trimak studied his behaviour closely, watching as he tried to get a reaction from Rachel.

'The boy seems himself,' said Trimak warily.

It took far longer for Morpeth to wake Rachel. Eventually she stirred, and the moment her eyes opened she leapt on Eric, tearing at his arms, screaming with frenzy. Startled, Eric managed to stagger away. Morpeth jumped on Rachel, holding her down.

'I'll kill you! I'll kill you, child!' Rachel shrieked at Eric.

'Stop her!' said Trimak. 'What's happening?'

Morpeth pinned Rachel's arms to the floor. 'I told you, Trimak. I told you how dangerous it would be to wake her before she was ready!'

Eric approached Rachel.

'Stay back,' warned Morpeth.

Eric touched one of her kicking feet. Instantly, Rachel stopped struggling. For a moment she seemed lost, then gazed at her hands, feeling them come back under her control.

'What's happening?' she asked. 'Eric . . . I didn't hurt you, did I?'

Morpeth stared at Eric. 'You broke the Witch's control over Rachel. How?'

Eric shrugged. 'I didn't do anything. I just grabbed her foot, that's all.'

'But she changed the *moment* you touched her.'

Rachel jumped up. She clutched Eric and moved them both away from Morpeth. 'Don't answer any of his questions,' she told Eric. 'He's working for the Witch.'

'That's not true,' Morpeth protested. 'I know it seems—'

'Why did you leave me in the eye-tower with Dragwena?' Rachel demanded. 'You knew what was going to happen inside, didn't you? You shut the door in my face.'

'I had no choice,' Morpeth said. 'Please try to understand. Dragwena watches all her servants so closely. If I had not dragged you all the way to the eye-tower, someone would have reported it. I had to appear merciless.'

'Why should I believe you?' Rachel said. 'How do I know you're not lying?'

Morpeth swept his arms around the cave. 'Look at this dark place,' he said. 'If I was a friend of the Witch do you think I'd bring you here? I'm risking my life doing this. So is Trimak.' He told her about the Sarren and their struggle against the Witch.

Rachel relaxed slightly. She explained about the snakes-and-ladders game and the dream of the Child Army and the Wizards. Both Morpeth and Trimak listened in fascination, never having heard this story before.

'Do you know what this means?' Morpeth whispered to Trimak.

Trimak nodded. 'It means the Witch has put her complete faith in Rachel. She will stop at nothing to recover the child.'

'Indeed, no place will be safe to hide her,' Morpeth said. 'We must protect Rachel in another way. We must work on her magic. She must learn how to defend *herself.*'

Rachel considered the meaning of her dream. 'At least I understand why Dragwena hates all children now,' she said. 'But I still don't know why she wants *me.*'

'The magic of children!' Morpeth exclaimed. 'Now it all makes sense! Dragwena has been bringing children to Ithrea for countless centuries, always testing, always hoping. From Rachel's dream we know the Wizards imprisoned the Witch here. All this time she must have been waiting for a single child with enough strength to help her get back. Rachel *is* that child!'

'But in the dream,' said Rachel, 'the Wizard Larpskendya told Dragwena she would always be alone, imprisoned forever on Ithrea. How did all the children get here?'

'If your dream is true,' said Morpeth, 'the Wizards made a mistake, or underestimated Dragwena. She long ago found a way to bring children from Earth.'

'The Wizard also mentioned he would develop magic in Earth's children, give them gifts to protect themselves if needed,' said Trimak. 'We have seen little evidence of that till you arrived, Rachel. Perhaps he meant you. You are to be our protection. You and Eric.'

'I can't do anything,' Eric said. 'Rachel's got all the magic.'

'But you smashed the Witch's control over your sister,' said Morpeth. 'Tell us how you did that.'

'I don't know,' Eric said. 'I just wanted Rachel back to normal. I didn't feel anything when it happened.'

'Mm,' Morpeth said, stroking his beard. 'What else do we know? The Wizard spoke about a song. What do you think he meant by it?'

'My song will always be on Ithrea,' Rachel whispered. 'That's what Larpskendya said. If I am called I will return.'

'Called how?' asked Morpeth. 'Called by whom?'

They sat for some time in the dark silence of the cave, pondering this.

'We're guessing at what the dream means,' Rachel said eventually. 'But I'm sure about one thing: Dragwena will search for me. Now she knows what I can do she'll never stop looking. You've betrayed her, Morpeth. She'll kill you and Trimak. Then she'll study Eric until she finds out how to use his gift.' She held her head erect, trembling slightly. 'I know what she'll do with me – turn me into her little Witch. It shouldn't be hard. I tried to stop her in the tower. I was useless.'

'Not useless,' Morpeth reassured her. 'You need training, to develop your spells and sharpen your magic. Then you'll be ready to face Dragwena.'

'I might never be strong enough,' said Rachel. 'I know what Dragwena's like. If she can't use me, she'll *kill* me. I'm too dangerous to live as her enemy.' She looked fiercely at Morpeth. 'I'm right, aren't I?'

'Perhaps,' Morpeth said. 'However, I believe that you are stronger than you realize; and I also believe that Dragwena can be defeated because she makes mistakes.'

'What mistakes?'

'She allowed you to slip from her grasp. That was foolish. She also trusted you with her deepest secrets too soon, when we – or Eric – could still reach into your mind and bring you back. And Dragwena does not realize I am a traitor. I've concealed my genuine thoughts for many years.'

'I wonder how well you know her,' Rachel said bluntly. 'I doubt you could hide your treachery for long. I don't think Dragwena makes mistakes. Perhaps she *let* me and Eric escape for some reason. Did you think of that?'

'Yes,' said Morpeth. 'We've considered it, but can think of no reason why the Witch would let you go so easily.'

Rachel made her fingernails glow bronze. 'Look at me,' she said. 'All this magic I've got. It's so strange. If I've got magic here why didn't I notice it at home? Why can't I use it there, too? It doesn't make sense.'

'All children have some magic on Ithrea,' said Morpeth.

'Dragwena is able to sense it when she draws children from Earth, so it must exist inside them there in some fashion. I've no idea why it can't be used.'

'Perhaps the Wizards don't allow it,' said Eric. 'They think it's too dangerous to use.'

Morpeth nodded thoughtfully. 'Have you ever seen the Wizards?'

'No,' Eric said. 'Have you?'

'No, nor anyone else on Ithrea,' said Morpeth. 'But I'd certainly like to meet the one called Larpskendya. I've got some good questions to ask him.'

Eric felt Trimak's beard. 'Hey, how old are you, anyway?'

'Pretty ancient,' sighed Trimak. 'Have a guess.'

'Eighty-six!'

Trimak laughed. 'Try again.'

'Younger or older?'

'Much older.'

'All right, a hundred and eighty-six!'

'Actually,' said Trimak, 'I am exactly five hundred and thirty-six years of age.'

Eric gasped. 'You can't be *that* old. You would be dead by now.'

'The Witch's power is responsible,' said Trimak. 'We have a saying here: she preserves those who serve. It helps keep her closest servants loyal. Morpeth is nearly as old as I am.'

'You were both stolen by the Witch from Earth, weren't you?' said Rachel. 'You are children who've grown up here.'

'Yes,' said Morpeth. 'Everyone on Ithrea was snatched away in a similar way to you and Eric. Dragwena does not let us grow gracefully into adults. I think she enjoys watching us get older and uglier in the same way together, until we have lost all our original features. The Witch also stunts our growth. It is as if she wishes to remind us we will always be children in her domain.'

'How many children live on Ithrea?' Rachel asked.

'Thousands have been abducted,' Morpeth answered. 'Some live around the Palace, those with the brightest magic, directly serving the Witch. Others are scattered around the planet.'

'But how can they live in this cold?' Rachel asked. 'How do they survive?'

'They live underground,' said Morpeth. 'They dig tunnels. They exist as best they can.'

Eric shook his head. 'But what do they eat? How do they grow anything?'

Morpeth grunted. 'Nothing much grows on Ithrea. They hunt for what meat they can find. Mostly burrowing worms. There aren't many. They cultivate a few herbs. They survive somehow on this, or die trying.' He glanced awkwardly at Trimak. 'Every year, from all over Ithrea, they make the trek across the storms and snows to the Palace. Dragwena insists they bring food for us.'

'For *you*?' said Eric.

Morpeth rubbed his round stomach. 'Yes. Dragwena could easily provide all we need, but she likes to watch the others struggle to bring the food here. She forces her Palace servants to eat, knowing it means all the others starve. Dragwena likes it that way.'

Rachel touched him gently on the shoulder. 'Does the Witch ever allow you . . . to die?'

'All the original children are now dead,' said Morpeth. 'Anyone who resists the Witch is killed immediately unless, like you, Rachel, they show promise. Sometimes Dragwena casts them out to the wolf packs, or she just leaves them to succumb to the cold. Perhaps those are the lucky children. Finally, the Witch kills us all, either because we grow too old to be useful or simply because she grows bored with us. No one dies naturally of old age on Ithrea. Dragwena is always there at the end of our lives, causing the final pain, enjoying the moment.'

Rachel and Eric fell silent.

'When I touched Dragwena's mind in the eye-tower,' Rachel said at last, 'I sensed there had been others like the Sarren in the past. Those who have tried to resist secretly. I think Dragwena actually wants you to rebel. I think she enjoys the challenge of letting you become a pest, then stamping you out. It's all just a game to her.'

'You may be right,' said Trimak hoarsely. 'But I'm certain the Witch has never faced a child such as you before, Rachel. She has never faced the child-hope.'

'*That* again,' said Rachel. 'What is this child-hope you and Morpeth keep talking about? Tell me.'

Morpeth glanced anxiously at Trimak, who nodded.

'The child-hope is a legend,' said Morpeth. 'That's all. No one knows where it came from, nor what it truly means, but it has been passed from generation to generation on Ithrea, even amongst the Neutrana. It tells of a dark girl-child who will come to free us all. The legend has grown over the centuries, but the original verse from which it springs is short enough:

'Dark girl she will be,
Enemies to set free,
Sing in harmony,
From sleep and dawn-bright sea,
I will arise—'

'And behold your childish glee,' Eric finished.

Everyone turned towards him.

'How do you know the end of the verse?' gasped Morpeth.

'I don't know,' said Eric, looking bewildered.

'Someone must have told you,' said Trimak.

Eric shrugged. 'I've never heard the words before. They just came into my head.'

Morpeth looked expectantly at Rachel.

'I don't recognize them at all,' she said. 'The words are so . . . strange. What do they mean?'

'Who knows?' Morpeth said bitterly. 'Perhaps nothing. Perhaps everything. Your hair is dark, your powers beyond anything we've seen before. We hoped *you* would know what they meant.'

'I know what some of it means,' Eric said.

'Tell us,' breathed Trimak.

Eric appeared almost bashful, as if the words held him in awe.

'*Enemies to set free,*' Rachel whispered. 'Are we the enemies?'

'No,' said Eric. 'Neutrana.'

Morpeth trembled. 'What about the last part of the verse? What or who will arise from sleep and dawn-bright sea? Do you know?'

Eric's face lit up. In a purely childlike way Rachel had not seen in him since he was a young boy he flapped his arms. '*Whoosh*!' he crooned, running in circles around the cave. 'Whoosh! Whoosh!'

Everyone watched Eric in fascination. Eventually he calmed down and came back, looking sheepish.

'What was all that about?' Rachel asked. 'Were you supposed to be flying?'

'No,' Eric said. 'I mean – yes, I might have been. Oh, I don't know!'

'What does *sing in harmony* mean?' Morpeth asked.

'Beats me,' Eric muttered, looking uncomfortable under their stares.

'*Beats me*?' Rachel said. 'Come on, Eric, you're not taking this seriously.'

'Yes, I am!'

'Be honest,' she said. 'Did someone tell you this verse before? Better let me know quick if you're faking it.'

'I'm not faking it!'

Rachel sat down until her eyes were on a level with his. 'All right,' she said. 'I believe you. Think a minute. In my dream the Wizard Larpskendya told Dragwena his song will always be on Ithrea. Do you know what that means?'

'No, I don't,' Eric said angrily. 'Stop getting at me.'

Rachel turned in frustration to Morpeth. 'I suppose you think I'm the one to free everyone. You think I'm your precious child-hope. Are all your hopes about me based on this little verse? A few lines about a dark child?'

'Yes,' said Morpeth. 'Exactly.'

'But the words of the verse . . . well, they could mean almost anything!'

Morpeth grinned. Wrinkles deep enough to snuggle inside appeared under his eyes and criss-crossed his sunken cheeks. 'Don't you understand?' he cried. 'Until now they could have meant anything. But *Eric* knows the words! Apart from myself, the only contact he's had on Ithrea is with Dragwena – and I'm sure the Witch would never have put these ideas into his head.'

'I'm scared,' Eric whispered.

'Of the verse?' Rachel asked.

'No. I'm scared of Dragwena.' He murmured this. Rachel knew how hard it was for him to admit it, especially in front of Morpeth and Trimak.

'So am I,' Rachel said. 'But I'm sick of being scared of her, aren't you?'

Eric nodded fervently.

Rachel turned to Morpeth and Trimak. 'I'm not sure if this verse means anything,' she said. 'But I bet Dragwena already knows we've been kidnapped. We can't have much time before she finds us. You told me that if I learned some new spells I might be able to fight her.'

'We'll begin your training at once,' said Morpeth. 'Eric can stay with Trimak.'

'No,' Rachel said. 'Eric and I stay together.'

'It's too dangerous,' warned Trimak. 'Dragwena will use him as a weapon against you.'

'I won't do anything unless you agree,' Rachel said flatly.

'It's too risky,' said Morpeth. 'We can protect Eric better if you are separated.'

'You have no idea how to protect him,' Rachel said. 'Stop

pretending you do. I can probably take care of Eric better than all the Sarren. You should know that by now.'

'Very well,' said Morpeth gloomily. 'Follow me.'

11

MAGIC

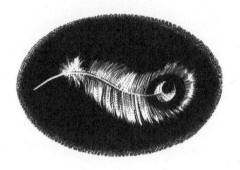

Morpeth led Rachel and Eric from Worraft. For some time they shuffled in silence under a low ceiling of cold corridors. As Morpeth padded along, red doors winked alight ahead of his footsteps, extinguishing the moment he passed. Occasionally he took them through one of the red doors. Each door always led to another almost identical corridor and more doors, in a seemingly endless series of upward sharp bends.

Rachel felt dizzy. 'How do you know the way?'

'Magic. This was built many years ago, the secret labour of a few Sarren. Dragwena knows nothing of it. You are the first children to come here.'

'Where are we going?' asked Eric, gazing round intently.

'To my study.' Morpeth stopped outside a door which looked like all the others. 'Now do you think you can remember how to find your way here from Worraft?'

Rachel looked at Eric and they both shook their heads.

'Good,' said Morpeth. 'Only a special kind of magic can guide you this way again.'

'Could the Witch find us?' Rachel said.

'In time she could. She would have to find Worraft first. There is no other way in here, and Dragwena does not even know about the cave. At least, I hope not.'

He blew on the door three times to open it and ushered the children inside.

Morpeth's 'study' was nothing more than a cramped oblong room, with a simple bed, a table and a single chair.

'What can you do to help me fight the Witch?' Rachel asked Morpeth. 'You know so many spells, and—'

'Me?' He laughed. 'I nearly collapsed just trying to keep up with you at breakfast!'

'What do you mean?'

'Do you remember those fish earrings? I had to use *all* of my power to alter their colour!'

Rachel gasped. 'I wondered why they kept changing!'

'You also played snakes and ladders against Dragwena and won. All children who have taken that test have failed: every one of them.' He put his hands on Rachel's shoulders. 'You *are* the child-hope. I'm sure of it.'

'But how can I defeat the Witch? What do I have to do?'

'You need to learn some new spells,' Morpeth said. 'You also need to practise. Dragwena has practised for centuries. When she commands, she is instantly obeyed. She can change shape in a moment.'

'But it's *hard* to change shape,' Rachel said dejectedly. 'I only did it because I was scared. What do I have to become to defeat Dragwena?'

'I don't know,' said Morpeth.

Rachel stared at him. 'I can't believe it. You expect *me* to know!'

'Well,' he said, 'let's not worry about confronting Dragwena for now. One step at a time. Will you play a magic game with me?'

Rachel sighed, recalling the sheer joy of making magic in the Breakfast Room, smashing melons into walls. Magic no longer seemed like a game.

Eric parked himself comfortably on Morpeth's bed and watched.

'I want you to try changing your shape again,' Morpeth said. 'What would be a clever disguise on Ithrea?'

'A snowflake,' Rachel answered at once. She quickly pictured herself as a snowflake drifting in the air. 'Well?'

'Same skinny legs as always,' said Eric.

'Don't be concerned,' Morpeth told her. 'It's much harder than you think. When we played in the Breakfast Room and rode over the mountains Dragwena put a special blanket of magic around us. But you soon began using your own magic. When you flew to the lake and changed into the feather, the Witch's magic didn't help you. You did those things yourself. You can do that here, now, but you must concentrate fully. Using real magic is extremely dangerous and requires all your attention.'

Rachel glanced around the room. 'Can I try to be something different? I don't really want to be a snowflake. I'd rather be a horse – or something that's *alive*.'

'A horse, however lovely, would hardly fit into this

study,' said Morpeth drily. 'I want you to fight against the desire to become just *anything*. You need to be more disciplined in your use of power.'

'I don't understand.'

'When you changed into a feather it saved your life,' he explained. 'You see, it is because you became what you needed to be, what you *had* to be at that instant. Dragwena will give you little chance to think when she attacks. You may be able to save us all if you can, at the moment of danger, change into the *right thing*, whatever that is. Now try to concentrate.'

Rachel forced herself to relax, to focus on the snowflake image. She ran fingers of ice over her body, colder, colder, until her brittle eyelids froze against the pupils. Shape next. Skin folding, bones condensing, until she shrunk to the size of a palm, then a finger, a thumbnail; then smaller still, so tiny she would hardly be noticed. She made her limbs and head disappear. She made her body fluffy and white, with sharp crystalline edges. It took an enormous effort, but for the first time Rachel was conscious that instead of instinctively reacting she could control the transformation herself. She blinked, opening her new snow eyes.

Morpeth and Eric had disappeared – at least Rachel thought so, before realizing she had been slowly drifting alongside Morpeth's trousers for several seconds. She landed gently on the floor. Hardness and dust pressed harshly against her. A few feet away Eric's giant shoe stepped back.

Before Rachel even had time to grow used to her snowflake-ness she noticed a pool of water surrounding her body. Am I bleeding? she wondered. Suddenly she understood: I'm not bleeding. I'm *melting*. I'm melting on the floor!

The next moment she had changed again: she was a drop of water.

Little currents of liquid lapped inside her new body from one side to the other.

Mm, she mused, no longer frightened, merely curious. A drop of water would be more interesting if she could . . . take off . . . like a plane!

Instantly she jerked from the floor, flying slowly at first, but speeding up as she learnt how to use her new wing-flaps. She hovered in mid air, gazing about. A few feet away Morpeth's nose loomed, as big as a bus. Rachel zoomed three fast circles over his head, then darted into Eric's ear, out again and over his cheeks, through his blond curls, onto his nose. A slide! She skied down the bridge of his nose and hung at the tip, swinging backwards and forwards. Looking up, she saw Eric's huge face gazing down from crossed eyes. Rachel flipped herself into a dive.

I'll allow myself to fall, she thought. I can't hurt myself. I'm just a splodge of water . . .

Her little body exploded as it hit the stone, splitting into hundreds of tiny water droplets that leapt away from the rest of her body. Panicking, Rachel tried to imagine herself as a girl again . . .

A deep voice – Morpeth's – blasted, '*No!* Stay as you are!'

Rachel waited anxiously. A moment later her tongue flew into the air. She watched her legs shoot upwards and wriggled her nose, a girl again.

'That was fantastic!' Rachel said. 'Can we do it again?'

Morpeth glared at her. '*You stupid girl,*' he roared. 'Do you know what would have happened if you had changed back when you were scattered all over the floor?'

'I—'

He gripped her arm. 'I'll tell you what would have happened: you would have come back as a girl in pieces! Your arms, legs and head would have been all over the room. *You would be dead!*'

'I'm – I'm sorry,' said Rachel. 'I didn't know. You didn't tell me.'

Morpeth sighed heavily. 'You see, when you change into another form you really *become* it.'

'I don't understand.'

'Think of a lizard. If you changed yourself into a lizard someone could chop off your tail and you could still crawl around, couldn't you?'

Rachel nodded.

'But if you changed back you might find one of your legs missing.' He grinned. 'I think I prefer girls with two legs, don't you?'

Rachel stared at the floor. 'I'll try to remember.'

'Good.' Morpeth flapped his arms. 'What a magnificent creature you became! I felt dizzy watching you shoot about.'

Rachel pointed at his face. 'What a big nose you have!'

Morpeth rubbed his thick nose playfully. 'I dread to think how big it must appear to a drop of water! Let's play some more.'

'First, why couldn't I change back to being me again?'

'It is much harder to change back to your real self,'

Morpeth explained. 'I don't know why. Only Dragwena is able to do it. However, when I saw you scattered all over the floor I sensed you might try.'

'*You* can change me back. You've done it twice now.'

'It's a gift from the Witch,' Morpeth said. 'Dragwena is always concerned there are enemies hiding inside everyday shapes like trees or birds or wolves. She gave me the power centuries ago to *unchange* things – to change them back to their true form. Until I reversed you back from the feather I did not know I could do it.'

'Why can't you change yourself into a feather or a snowflake?'

'That is a gift only you and Dragwena share,' Morpeth replied. 'You are the first child to have shape-shifted.' He gazed wistfully at her. 'You are the first to have done many things.'

'Maybe I'm a Witch,' Rachel said anxiously.

'I don't think so.' He smiled ruefully. 'Or, if you are a Witch, you are a very nice one.'

Eric lay down on Morpeth's bed and snuggled the pillow.

'Can I have a nap?' he asked, yawning. 'I'm really tired.'

'How can you be tired after what you've just seen?' said Morpeth. He looked puzzled, then relaxed again. 'I'm forgetting what a long night you had. Of course you can. I will wake—'

But Eric had already nodded off.

Once they were sure Eric was asleep, Rachel whispered to Morpeth: 'What will we do next?'

'Why not try being something more solid this time?' Morpeth said. He looked around the room. 'This place is a little bare, in my view. How about some more furniture?'

With a grin Rachel instantly transformed herself into a high-backed chair, with carved wooden legs.

'Can you hear me?' Morpeth asked.

'Yes,' she tried to reply, finding her mouth inside the wooden frame. She brought her lips onto the cushion, and placed her eyes above them. 'I can hear you perfectly!'

'Interesting,' he said. 'A chair that can talk. Whatever next?'

'A table!'

She lengthened her legs, made the cushion disappear, and transformed the seat into a big flat top.

'Hi,' she said breathlessly.

'Quite clever,' Morpeth said. 'Let's put you to a real test. Can you imagine you are *me*?'

'What? You mean make myself look like you?'

Morpeth nodded.

'I'll try,' said the little lips on the table.

Rachel observed Morpeth carefully, studying everything about him: his long arms, the flat bulbous line of his nose, the ancient sunken cheeks. She examined his leather clothes, trying to work out what the old garments must feel like to wear.

'Well?' she asked, rushing to finish.

'See for yourself,' said Morpeth, pointing to a small mirror on the wall.

Rachel dashed across expectantly. The creature staring back was a mess. The clothes were accurate, but Morpeth's beard was only half made and she had not even remembered to change his hair or square jaw. What looked back from the mirror was a crude Morpeth, with long dark hair and a pointed chin like her own.

She laughed – and realized Morpeth also had her small even teeth.

'Oh dear,' she said. 'I'm a sort of Rachel-Morpeth thing.'

The voice was also her high-pitched own. She had forgotten to change that as well.

'Mm,' Morpeth said. 'It's much harder to imagine being a person, isn't it? Tables and chairs don't have voices or teeth. You have to think carefully and remember everything about people, even the things you cannot see.'

'At least I got your nose right,' Rachel said, pressing it.

'That's not true,' said Morpeth. 'Your nose is much too big.'

Rachel checked in the mirror. 'No,' she said, twitching it. 'I think the nose is just like yours. It's exactly the right size.'

Morpeth frowned. 'Perhaps you're right.'

'Should I make the nose smaller? Would you like that?'

'Isn't it perfect already?' he asked. 'Oh, all right. Why not!'

Rachel made a snub nose. They looked in the mirror together.

'Not bad,' he said. 'But can you make me look *handsome*? There's a test for you!'

Rachel tried a few different combinations before she found what she wanted. The creature now standing next to Morpeth was a tall good-looking man with sandy hair and piercingly blue eyes.

Morpeth stared in astonishment. 'He is certainly more handsome. But does it look like me?'

'I don't know,' Rachel replied, uncertainly. 'I saw you as a boy in the dream Dragwena gave me. You look a bit like a grown-up version of him.'

'You may be right, Rachel,' he muttered, touching her face awkwardly. 'It has been so long since I was a boy. I had forgotten . . . what I used to be like.'

He stared sadly at the floor.

'I didn't mean to upset you,' she said. 'Perhaps . . . perhaps I can really make *you* look like this. Do you want me to?'

'I'm so old I don't care what I look like,' said Morpeth. 'Anyway, it is impossible—' He stopped and gazed sharply at Rachel. 'Go on then. Change me if you can!'

Rachel considered how to do it. How can I go *inside* him? she wondered. On impulse, she transformed into a speck of dust, so tiny that she could enter the pores of his skin. Small currents of air in the room moved her around. Rachel steadied herself, landed on his hair, felt the texture and dryness. She moved carefully among the strands sculpting them, made them lighter, silkier. Next she softened his cheeks, smoothed out the wrinkles and changed the colour of his eyes to a deeper blue. She made herself into a small pair of scissors to cut off his ragged beard. After several minutes of hard work she was finished – or almost. She reached into all his limbs, stretching out his body, making him taller. Feeling tired, she flew to the middle of the room and turned herself into a table again.

Morpeth sat in front of her, but not the wrinkled old dwarf Rachel knew. He was a tall young man, with curly thick hair and radiant blue eyes.

Morpeth gasped at his reflection in the mirror, pinching his face as if it were a mask. He blinked rapidly and his new blue eyes blinked back.

'You look very handsome now,' said the table.

'How did you do this?' he marvelled. 'You should not be able to change *someone else*. Only Dragwena has that power.'

'I don't know,' she said.

'Imagine you're Rachel again. Change yourself back,' Morpeth said firmly.

'You told me only Dragwena can do that.'

'That's what I used to believe. Now I am certain you can do it.'

Rachel knew what was needed at once. She saw herself as a girl again, wearing the soft leather of the Sarren. It was somehow easier than before. She did not even need to concentrate. Rachel walked confidently across the room to the mirror. A girl with large green eyes, a sharp nose and a small beauty spot on her left cheek peered back.

'I did it!'

Morpeth's jaw dropped open. Then he gazed at his own handsome face in the mirror, pulling faces to see his new expressions.

But Rachel had not finished. Suddenly ideas were occurring to her which even Morpeth could not have conceived. She pictured *another* Rachel in the room, placing it behind him. It stood there, as rigid as a plastic doll. She made it step forward. It moved stiffly, like a robot.

Rachel concentrated harder, gave it bones, ligaments and muscles that could move flexibly, like a real person. She made the second Rachel stretch out its arms and place small fingers around Morpeth's ears.

He gasped, jumping away.

'Which one is me?' asked both girls at the same time.

Rachel smiled and the fake girl smiled too.

Morpeth stared at both of them. At first they seemed identical. As he looked more closely he noticed that one of the girls had a slightly bland appearance. He grinned confidently at Rachel. '*You* are the real one.'

Rachel could also see the differences. She made the bland expression disappear.

'Which one is Rachel now?' asked both girls.

Morpeth studied each child closely. He touched their cheeks. He felt their hair. He picked them up. They were the same weight – Rachel had even considered that. Eventually, he shrugged.

'I don't know,' he said. 'I can't tell which is real. You *both* look real.'

Rachel giggled and wished the second Rachel to vanish. It disappeared at once.

Morpeth sat down heavily on a chair, and they stared in silence at each other.

'I – I don't know what to say,' he said. 'The things you are doing should not be possible. I have no idea how you've done them.'

'I can teach you,' Rachel said. 'It's not hard.'

Morpeth rubbed his handsome new chin. 'I am supposed to be teaching *you*,' he grunted. 'I see instead I have much to learn! I think—'

A noise from the bed distracted them both. It was Eric, talking in his sleep.

'He must be dreaming,' said Rachel.

'Shush! Listen to what he's saying.'

Eric twisted in the bed. 'Fifteen,' he said. 'Left. Eight. Right. Four. Left. Six. Left. Two.' He continued to say the strange numbers.

'What's he muttering?' Rachel asked. 'It sounds like a weird dream.'

'It's not a dream!' Morpeth jumped up. 'It is the way to this room through the corridors and doors. *Dragwena is coming.*'

'What do you mean?' Rachel cried. 'You said Dragwena wouldn't be able to find us?'

'Don't you see?' he said. 'The Witch has tricked us all. She was alone with your brother for several hours. She must have planted a finding spell within him!'

Rachel put her hand across Eric's mouth. Still asleep, possessing extraordinary strength, he ripped the hand away.

'Right. Four. Left. Six. Right. Two.'

Rachel burst into tears. 'Can't we stop him?'

'There's no time!'

Morpeth pressed a spot on the floor and a small exit appeared in one of the walls.

'Quick,' he said. 'We must leave at once!'

'But we can't leave Eric here,' Rachel insisted. 'We have to take him with us.'

'No!' Morpeth leapt towards the exit. 'He is under Dragwena's control. We can't help him now. Come with me.'

He jumped through the exit and held out his hand.

'I won't go without Eric,' Rachel shouted. 'I'm not leaving him!' As she tried to pick Eric up he kicked out savagely in his sleep. 'C'mon,' Rachel snarled. 'You're coming whether you want to or not!' She dragged Eric across to the exit into Morpeth's reluctant arms.

'We *can't* take him with us,' Morpeth said desperately. 'You must understand, Rachel. He's Dragwena's slave now! Leave, before it's too late!'

'Not without Eric!'

With no time to argue, Morpeth clutched Eric with one arm, reaching with the other for Rachel. 'I've got him! Now follow! Hurry!'

Rachel took a step forward, but a blast of wind startled her. The main door leading to the room had been smashed open.

In the doorway stood Dragwena.

The Witch glanced at Morpeth's escape exit, slamming it shut. Rachel heard him running away down the tunnel, calling 'See you at Hoy Point! *Hoy Point!*' as the sound of his footsteps disappeared.

Two Neutrana guards leapt into the room alongside the Witch.

'You must open the exit,' one said. 'Let us kill Morpeth.'

'No,' Dragwena answered. 'He can't escape. We'll deal with him later.'

Rachel wasted no time. She pictured herself as a sword, flying towards the Witch's head, but before she could complete the thought Dragwena knocked her to the ground.

'Tut, tut,' Dragwena scoffed. 'What nonsense has Morpeth been teaching you? My magic is stronger than anything he knows. Do you think you can challenge me, child? Did you believe I would ever allow you to escape?'

'I won't let you use me to harm anyone,' shouted Rachel. 'You'll have to kill me first, Witch. My magic's getting stronger. I can fight you now!'

With two fingers Dragwena wrenched Rachel from the floor, as if she weighed nothing.

'Soon you will want to be with me forever,' Dragwena said. 'You will not want to fight. You will forget everyone else. I will suck them all from your mind.'

'I *hate* you!' Rachel struggled to free herself. 'You brought us here, didn't you? The black claws in the cellar were yours!'

The Witch smiled appreciatively. 'I am indeed the claws and many other things unspoken on this world. None of this will matter soon. I will change you into my own creature.' She stroked Rachel's hair. 'You will kill lots of children and, I promise, you will *enjoy* it.'

Tucking Rachel under her arm the Witch flew rapidly from the room and along the corridor. All the doors opened before her. Rachel tried to imagine herself by the shore of Lake Ker again. Each time she did so a wave of pain smashed her mind, scattering her thoughts. The Witch would not let her concentrate for a second.

Within moments they were out of the corridors and into Worraft, through the entrance and heading upwards. Freezing wind struck Rachel's face and she realized she was outside. The stars shot past her head. She arched her back and looked up. Ahead, the luminous green window of the eye-tower raced towards them.

12

the kiss breath

After Dragwena shut the escape exit Morpeth ran for his life carrying Eric, still half-asleep, down the narrow tunnel. A few moments later he stopped to listen, holding his breath, expecting to be chased by Dragwena and an army of Neutrana. Hearing nothing, he collapsed on the floor, safe for a moment at least.

You fool, he raged at himself, thumping the wall. You were supposed to protect her. Now Dragwena has Rachel and you will never get her back!

Eric, now wide awake, watched him fearfully.

'What happened?' he asked. 'Where's Rachel?'

Morpeth pressed his thumbs against Eric's temple, but felt no trace of Dragwena's magic left inside. The spell Dragwena planted, he now understood, must have been shallow, snapping as soon as Eric awakened. Morpeth groaned. Why hadn't he thought to check the boy properly earlier? Eric was the perfect spy, a neat snare leading Dragwena to Rachel and the Sarren. All along, he thought, perhaps long before Rachel arrived, Dragwena must have recognized his treachery. The Witch had used Rachel and Eric to flush out the secret locations of the Sarren, trapping them together under the Palace – a place they could easily be slaughtered.

I was too confident, he realized. I believed I could conceal my thoughts from the Witch. Rachel knew I was wrong!

He forced himself to calm down, knowing he needed help quickly if there was to be any hope of recapturing her. Picking Eric up he headed swiftly down to the deep caves where Trimak was hiding. As he got closer he heard anguished sounds – the screams of men and the ring of metal.

A fight was taking place.

Morpeth padded towards the sounds and drew his own short narrow sword. He had never used it before in a real battle. He had not bothered to sharpen it for years. Beyond a final door he could hear voices clearly now. A deep voice, Trimak's, barked desperate orders.

'We must go inside,' Morpeth told Eric. 'I may not be able to protect you if I have to fight in hand-to-hand combat. Stay behind me, close. If I'm injured you must find other Sarren to look after you as best they can. Do you understand?'

Eric nodded his head, intensely frightened.

Morpeth thought bitterly: thanks to my stupidity there is no safe place for you now, boy.

He pulled Eric against his back and put his shoulder against the door.

He gripped the haft of his sword tightly.

And leapt into the battle.

Rachel was held in the black arm-claw of the Witch, flying towards the eye-tower. A sharp wind tugged at her hair as she flew upward, the other Palace buildings disappearing below. Dragwena's face glowed in ecstasy. She held Rachel with one bent arm; the other arm pointed in front like a gun-barrel, slicing through the night air.

Rachel knew time was running out. She tried using her magic to slide from the Witch's grasp. But every time she began forming a spell snake-hairs burst from the Witch's head, smothering her face, breaking her concentration.

'Do you think your child-magic can affect a true Witch?' said Dragwena. 'I command all the magic on this world. Nothing you do could ever harm me.'

Rachel kicked out, thrashing helplessly in the grip of the Witch's claw.

Dragwena soared upward, the green window of the eye-tower looming. They flew straight into the glass. Rachel expected to be cut to pieces. But the glass did not shatter. It simply liquefied for a second as they entered.

Once they were inside Dragwena threw Rachel down on the floor. She bled slightly where the Witch's nails had dug into her back. She ignored the pain, glancing towards the window, ready to leap out, but the thick green glass had re-formed.

There was a timid knock on the door.

'Enter,' growled Dragwena.

Three Neutrana soldiers hesitantly set foot in the room and bowed.

'What news of Morpeth?' asked Dragwena.

'There is no news of the scum yet,' said one of the men. 'He can't hide for long. Our men are fighting the remaining Sarren. We have ten times their number. Guards are placed on all the cave exits. We are hunting them down, one by one.'

Dragwena rubbed her hands, her expression gleeful.

'Kill them all,' she said. 'I want every single rebel found and destroyed. Burn their bodies. Round up their families, along with anyone suspected of helping them. There will be no more Sarren.' She spat at the Neutrana soldier. 'I will teach your people a lesson they will never forget!'

He nodded uneasily and turned to leave.

'Wait!' snapped Dragwena. 'Tell your men there will be a special reward if Morpeth's head is brought to me before the end of the day. I want the traitor found. If I read the child before me correctly, he will be taller than anyone you have seen before, handsome, with – ah! – bright blue eyes. Ensure they are torn out while he's still alive.'

The Witch relaxed slightly, put her arms by her side, and indicated Rachel. 'Listen closely,' she hissed. 'The girl and I are not to be distracted for the next hour. Inform your guards and my servants. *Under no circumstances* must we be disturbed.'

As soon as the Neutrana soldiers left the Witch leapt across the room and slapped Rachel hard across the face.

'Now, child,' she said. 'There have been enough games played with Morpeth and his friends. They will all soon be dead, if they are not already. I have delayed long enough. It's time to turn you into something more useful.'

Rachel dragged herself away across the chamber.

Dragwena followed her in a leisurely way. 'I think we should improve your appearance,' she said. 'Where should we start? Those small teeth of yours, perhaps.'

All four jaws of the Witch lunged at Rachel.

Morpeth dashed through the doorway. The cave was full of armed Neutrana, trained soldiers of the Witch. A few lay dead on the cave floor, but the number of dead or wounded Sarren were much greater – they had not expected a fight and most had no weapons. The Neutrana, knowing no mercy, were tearing them to pieces. Trimak stood in a defensive line with the small group of Sarren who did possess swords. Morpeth saw dozens of fresh Neutrana troops entering the cave from both ends.

'Over here!' he barked. 'There is an escape route!'

'What?' said Trimak, squinting in the dim cave light while trying to fight. 'Who are you?'

'Morpeth! Trust your instinct!'

Trimak looked at the man – not Morpeth, though it spoke with his harsh voice.

'It *is* me,' Morpeth shouted. 'Rachel changed my appearance!'

Trimak uncertainly ordered the Sarren to follow the stranger.

The few Sarren who were not already cut off followed the command at once, dashing across the cave. A great roar of alarm came from the Neutrana and they surged towards

Morpeth. Four heavily armed Sarren fought furiously to keep them back.

'You go!' one cried to Trimak. 'We'll hold them off for as long as we can.'

'No, Grimwold,' Trimak shouted. 'We must all leave! Now is not the time to sacrifice your life.'

'If *this* is not a good time, then what is?' Grimwold bellowed. A Neutrana blade cut deeply into his cheek. He ignored it, screaming at the Witch's soldiers. 'Come on then, try your best! I'll fight you all!'

'Follow your orders!' Trimak commanded.

The last Sarren slipped through the doorway opened by Morpeth. Once they had escaped Grimwold lifted his free arm, making a slashing movement above his head.

Instantly his own men leapt towards the door.

Trimak drew it shut. Inside the narrow tunnel were eight Sarren left with Morpeth, Eric and Trimak. All the other Sarren were dead or had escaped elsewhere. The survivors sat in exhaustion, breathing heavily, some noticing their injuries for the first time now the battle had ceased. From the cave the Neutrana hurled their bodies at the door.

'It will not take them long to break through,' murmured one the Sarren.

Trimak turned to Morpeth. 'If you are really Morpeth,' he said, 'you will be able to seal the door.'

Morpeth opened his right palm towards the entrance, slowly melting the stonework until hardened rock smothered the doorway.

Even Grimwold, who was not easily impressed, looked in surprise at the sandy-haired man. 'The Morpeth I know is an ugly old devil,' he said. 'You must tell us who made you so handsome. I'd like to pay them a visit!'

'Where's Rachel?' asked Trimak.

'Dragwena found us,' said Morpeth. 'I couldn't stop her.'

'Then we must recapture the girl!' barked Grimwold. 'Does this tunnel lead anywhere?'

'It leads to many places,' said Morpeth. 'Most of the exits will be guarded. However, there is one route only I and Dragwena know about. It leads directly to the eye-tower. If we act quickly I think a small group could reach it.'

'The Witch's guards will be swarming about the eye-tower,' Trimak protested. 'Particularly at a time like this.'

'I doubt there will be many,' said Morpeth. 'The last thing Dragwena will suspect is an attack now. Especially an attack against her. Most of the Neutrana soldiers are still in the caves. There are probably few in the Palace itself.'

'What are we waiting for?' said Grimwold. 'I have wanted to kill that hag for so long.'

'Our aim must be to free Rachel,' Morpeth said. 'Dragwena would relish a direct fight. Somehow we must distract her.'

'Perhaps the Witch will be leading the battle in the caves,' suggested one of the Sarren.

Morpeth said quietly, 'No. Dragwena knows that battle is already won. She will work on Rachel immediately. The dream-sleep will already have half-prepared the child. Rachel did not have nearly enough time with me to develop her defences. It won't take the Witch long to break her.'

The Sarren picked up their weapons and solemnly made their way up the winding tunnel.

*

Inside the eye-tower Dragwena smiled at Rachel.

Then she took a narrow pointed blade from her dress and jabbed Rachel's palm.

Rachel jumped back, clenching her hand. 'What have you done?'

Dragwena's four sets of teeth grinned together. 'I have started the transforming spell. You will soon begin to look like me.'

The Witch glided across the room and lit a long tapered candle. Engraved on the candle was a circle, and inside it a five-pointed star. The flame flickered with a cold green light. The Witch retired to a chair, leaving Rachel standing alone in the middle of the chamber. For a few minutes they simply gazed at one another without speaking, the Witch kissing the head of her snake, while Rachel rubbed her hand, trying to decide what to do. She could hear a few people passing outside the corridor, whispering commands. Behind her the green window of the eye-tower stared down at the Palace buildings, but she knew there was no hope of escape in that direction.

Inexplicably, Rachel found herself relaxing. The wound in her hand no longer hurt. She breathed deeply. The candle gave off a delicious perfume. She sniffed the air, vaguely aware that most of the smoke was drifting towards her nose and mouth. She yawned – and flinched. Why was she tired? She blinked heavily, fighting to stay awake, recognizing the feeling from her last visit to the eye-tower yet unable to fight it, just as she had been unable to fight it before.

Dragwena's snake uncoiled slowly from her neck and lifted its head. Rachel tried in vain to turn her face away.

The snake moved lazily back and forth, tasting her eyelids with its tongue. Finally, Rachel could not prevent her lids from closing. With a huge effort she parted her lips, the sound taking an eternity to emerge.

'What – is – happening – to – me?'

'Happening?' replied Dragwena easily. 'Nothing is happening. We are simply sitting quietly, you and I together.'

Rachel fought to regain control of her mind. I have to stop breathing the smoke, she knew. I must put the candle out. She urged her frozen muscles to move.

At last she realized she did not *want* to move. Any thought of resisting the Witch had gone. A pleasant warmth spread up through her neck and shoulders. Her throat and lips tingled. She relaxed completely, forgetting Eric and the Sarren and the Witch. She lay on the floor and drifted into sleep. When she awoke the room was unchanged. Dragwena gazed kindly, the snake once again coiled around her neck.

'There we are,' said Dragwena. 'Do you feel better now?'

Rachel tried to nod her head.

'You see,' said Dragwena gently, 'I am not such a terrible creature after all.'

Terrible creature? Rachel wondered vaguely what she meant.

'We can talk if you like,' Dragwena said. 'We can speak with our minds.'

'Mm.'

Dragwena's lips were shut. 'Can you hear me?'

'Yes.'

'Do you remember your friends?'

The image of some children came into Rachel's mind. She did not recognize them.

'Do you remember the Sarren who kidnapped you?'

Sarren? The name meant nothing, though it hardly mattered to Rachel. All that mattered was to listen to the lilting voice of the woman.

'These Sarren told some lies about me,' the Witch said. 'They also tried to kill you. I rescued you when Morpeth tried to kill you. Do you remember? Do you remember when he tried to kill you?'

An image leapt into Rachel's mind of a dwarf holding a knife against her throat. She saw Dragwena rush over to knock the knife out of his hand.

Rachel smiled inwardly. 'Thank you.'

'You are welcome,' replied Dragwena, pausing, knowing Rachel was already within her power, needing only to be given a new purpose for her remarkable gifts.

'You are a special child,' Dragwena explained. 'I want you to be with me forever. We will rule together, you and I. My kingdom is so large. I will need your help. Look for yourself—'

Suddenly, Rachel saw herself flying through the silence of deep space. A vast sun blazed at her back and crowns of stars clustered around her neck and shoulders. She wore a black dress and when she lifted her neck a snake with ruby-red eyes caressed her chin. Rachel peered down. Below her, a small planet swirled with white clouds and sparkling blue oceans. She flew effortlessly towards it, sensing neither wind nor cold, skimming its seas and streams and soaring with outstretched arms across mountains and plains. And wherever she flew huge armies of children followed, fighting for places to watch her pass and shout her name.

'Rachel! Rachel!' they chanted, raising their keen-edged swords.

She felt a soft touch on her hand. Dragwena flew alongside her, fingertip to fingertip.

'Will you rule with me?' Dragwena asked.

Rachel realized blissfully there was nothing else she would rather do. She smiled as her own snake embraced Dragwena's in the formal greeting of Witches . . .

At that moment a scuffle outside the eye-tower distracted Dragwena. Neutrana guards, caught unawares, leapt to protect the chamber. There followed a short fierce struggle, immediately shattered by a cry of Sarren as they threw their bodies at the thick chamber door.

Rachel, still in the bliss-trance of the Witch, paid no attention.

The door reverberated as it was repeatedly hit. At last, even the great hinges of the chamber could no longer bear the onslaught and the frame came shattering down. As it did so a blast of cold air shot into the room, snuffing out the candle.

Rachel awoke gradually from her daze and glanced at the doorway.

Standing there, flanked on either side by his men, was Grimwold.

In one arm he held a huge sword; in the other a knife. Both were covered in blood. Dead Neutrana of the Witch lay outside.

'I've come to kill you, Dragwena,' he hissed.

Dragwena gazed at their swords in amusement. 'Do you intend to kill me with those?' she asked. 'If you are to kill a High Witch they must be magic swords, blessed by magicians themselves. Did you know that?'

'I don't care!' Grimwold roared. 'I will kill you or die trying.'

All three Sarren leapt at her. Dragwena casually lifted a finger and a transparent green wall appeared between them. Grimwold charged the wall. As soon as the tip of his sword struck the surface it leapt into the Witch's palm. He watched in astonishment as Dragwena calmly tossed the blade aside.

'I think I have seen enough weapons today,' she said. 'Let me welcome you brave men in my own way.'

She pursed the thin lips covering her four sets of teeth and blew a gentle kiss towards them. As if in slow motion the kiss-breath left Dragwena's mouths and moved lazily towards the men. When it hit the transparent wall it quickly spread inside, twisting. The Sarren glanced at each other uncertainly.

Rachel had been desperately trying to find her voice.

'G-get out,' she stammered. 'Get out of the chamber!'

Grimwold stared at Rachel, noticing her for the first time.

'The child-hope,' he said, gazing in wonder.

Inside the wall the kiss-breath swirled angrily, preparing its attack.

'Leave now!' Rachel screamed. 'Run!'

'Too late,' sighed the Witch, laughing at the Sarren.

Grimwold suddenly understood. He dragged his men towards the open doorway, but as they turned the kiss-breath ripped through the transparent wall, slamming them against the stone floor of the corridor.

The Sarren lay in a crumpled heap on the floor, their swords broken.

'No!' Rachel wailed.

Dragwena ignored her and went over to inspect the men's bodies.

Rachel held back her tears, knowing this might be her only chance to escape. She had to alter quickly, while Dragwena was distracted. What should she change into? Something too small to be seen. Her mind raced. A speck of dust! Yes, it could work . . .

As she transformed she quickly placed another Rachel in the room. Dragwena was still examining the Sarren, a smile on her face. Good. She had not noticed. Rachel became a speck of near nothingness, incredibly light, so light the merest breeze picked her up. She floated, allowing it to carry her towards the open doorway of the chamber.

The Witch lost interest in the Sarren. She stared suspiciously at the fake Rachel.

'Speak to me!' Dragwena commanded it.

Rachel tried to make the dummy Rachel talk, but it was too hard to do this and imagine herself as a speck of dust at the same time. She floated slowly out of the doorway. Dragwena's eyes widened in sudden understanding. She reached inside her dress, pulled out a curved blade, and stabbed the fake Rachel in the heart.

The real Rachel screamed – a human scream, loud and agonized, revealing her position.

Almost fainting from the pain, Rachel gave herself little

wings and flapped down the steep winding stairway, searching frantically for a window. There had to be a way out . . .

A whoosh of air sighed above – Dragwena flew towards her. A large tongue emerged from the Witch's mouth, tasting the air, seeking Rachel's presence. At the same time an impulse thrust into Rachel's mind, suggesting she change back into a girl. She felt her dusty body start to alter.

No! Rachel thought furiously, holding her shape.

A window – closed, but there was a crack in the frame through which she could squeeze. For a second she was in darkness, then a wider darkness tinged with stars.

A snowflake struck her like an avalanche. Rachel collapsed inside, shaking with the effort to stop herself transforming back into a girl.

She glanced back. The window was open. Dragwena stood there, extending an arm. Rachel tried to leap away, but a giant claw closed around her. In a moment, Rachel knew, everything Morpeth had done, everything the Sarren had struggled and died for, would be for nothing.

No! No! she thought. I will escape. I *will!*

She remembered her race with Morpeth to the lake. She saw herself looking into its frozen waters, far from the eye-tower.

Her stomach tugged and when she dared to look it was not the face of Dragwena but the gleam of frost on the shore of Lake Ker which met her gaze. Behind her, a shriek of rage came distantly from the Palace as Dragwena clutched vainly in the air.

Rachel shuddered, snowflakes crushing her head. She had no strength left to bring her body back. The snow continued to fall steadily, burying her in soft, bitterly cold clumps.

I'll just lie here for a while, she told herself. I'll think of what to do soon. I'll . . .

Exhaustion closed her speck-of-dust eyes.

13

JOURNEY IN
the snow

It was a bright, crisp morning in Ithrea and a light wind hardly stirred the feathers of the great white eagle, Ronnocoden. A mile above the eye-tower he soared, wheeling in great circles, closely watching events below.

The giant central gates of the Palace were open. Pouring from them was a vast army of Neutrana sniffer-troops, dressed for a long journey. They headed northwards towards the Ragged Mountains. Many had recently fought with fury against the Sarren in the tunnels of the Palace. The Witch allowed them no rest, nor herself. All night she had worked on the spell she needed: the Neutrana troops spilling from the gates now had the soft, odour-sensitive muzzles of dogs, which they pressed low to the ground. Only one smell had their attention: the scent of magic –

Rachel's magic. They fanned out evenly on a wide track. Every now and then one would eagerly sniff the snow at its feet, excited by some trail or other, before moving restlessly on.

The eagle lifted his head, following the sniffer-troops beyond the range of normal vision, to the far north. There, amongst the mountains and valleys of the Ragged Mountains, he saw even more transformed Neutrana, and also other creatures: wolves. Each was the size of a black bear, with bright yellow eyes. Like giant outlandish dogs they loped around, pushing their muzzles into the snow. And amongst the wolves stood Dragwena, stroking them, encouraging them, guiding them where to look.

Ronnocoden silently dropped lower. His keen stone-grey pupils watched as a figure white-on-white shuffled slowly towards the edge of Lake Ker. Below, the shape paused, adjusted its cowl, and lifted blue eyes in recognition.

Instantly, Ronnocoden tipped a wing to indicate the gardens were safe from prying eyes. Then he flew rapidly southwards, disappearing within seconds into the high clouds.

The creature on the ground reached the brink of the lake. It pressed its face against the snow near a tree stump shaped like a mushroom, muttered two words and stepped back.

A girl shot into the air.

The creature hurriedly wrapped another white cloak around her body.

'Morpeth!' Rachel gasped.

'You are alive!' He rubbed her freezing cheeks. 'I feared the worst. I thought – how happy I am to see you!'

'Oh Morpeth,' said Rachel, between chattering teeth. 'I'm freezing. I was in the snow for ages. I couldn't change back.' She gazed around anxiously. 'Where's Eric?'

Morpeth reached inside the deep pockets of his cloak. He pulled out a small fur jacket, thick gloves, padded trousers and a pair of snowshoes matching those on his own feet. He placed a small knife in one of her pockets.

'Eric is safe,' he said. 'He made his way with Trimak to a cave network several miles south, called Latnap Deep. I'm to bring you there.'

'I tried to help the Sarren,' Rachel explained. 'I just didn't know what Dragwena planned to do. Then she blew that kiss, and . . .' She glanced up imploringly. 'Dragwena used Eric to find me, didn't she? Morpeth, please don't blame Eric. It's not his fault that—'

'I know,' Morpeth reassured her. 'Eric's his usual self again now.' He glanced over the Palace gardens. 'Sooner or later one of Dragwena's sniffer-troops will pick up your scent. We must be a long way from here when it does.'

'Mm,' said Rachel, peering under her cloak. 'How do we get to these caves? By using magic?'

'I wish we could! But my magic's not strong enough to take us. Only you can zip about from place to place like Dragwena. I have to walk about on my stubby old legs.'

'I'll carry you with me,' Rachel said. 'I'm sure I can do it. We'll fly to Latnap Deep together.'

'Try imagining yourself just a few feet away,' said Morpeth. 'Keep the cloak around you. We mustn't be seen.'

'I've lost my magic!' Rachel whispered, after several tries.

'No, you're simply exhausted after using so much energy escaping from Dragwena. A rest will do the trick, but it might take several hours to fully recover. We'll have to go on foot.' He helped her put on the snowshoes. 'The Witch is frightened now. She can't believe you outwitted her!'

'She never looks frightened,' said Rachel, remembering the ease with which Dragwena had greeted Grimwold and his men in her chamber. 'She can't really be scared of me.'

'Oh, she is! The Witch has been searching madly since dawn. Fortunately, she thinks you are in the Ragged Mountains. I have never known her to become personally involved in a search.' He grinned. 'She must be extremely worried.'

'Why does she think I'd be there?'

'Remember when I left the room and said, "See you at Hoy Point"?'

Rachel nodded.

'It's a peak in the mountains. I never expected Dragwena to believe it. I only said it in the hope of misleading her in case you managed to escape.' Morpeth chuckled. 'It seems to have worked, at least long enough to delay her for a short while.'

'How did you know where I was? I thought no one except Dragwena could find me.'

'I guessed if you were in danger you would return to this spot. It's the place you flew to on our first morning together. Of course,' he said, 'you could have turned up in the Breakfast Room, or your bedroom in the Palace – but I gambled you would never go somewhere Dragwena could easily find you.'

'I never thought about it,' Rachel said honestly. 'I didn't have time.'

'Then we must be grateful to Dragwena at least for that!'

He carefully tucked Rachel's scarf about her neck and assessed her with a new purposefulness. 'Let's go. It is a long journey to Latnap Deep on foot. I had planned for the eagles to carry us there, but the sky is so clear that Dragwena's spies would certainly spot us. We can't take that risk.'

'How can you be sure Dragwena doesn't know about these caves?'

'I can't be certain,' Morpeth admitted. 'But Latnap Deep has never been used in my lifetime by the Sarren. We are relying on that.'

Morpeth pointed across Lake Ker to a distant wood shrouded in mist. 'We're going that way,' he said. 'Walk close to me. The ice is thin in places, and the wolves will not so easily spot our tracks.'

'Wolves?'

'I'll tell you about them as we go,' said Morpeth.

He gripped her hand, preparing to set off.

'*Ouch!*' Rachel cried. She looked down. In the middle of her palm a black puncture wound throbbed painfully.

'Dragwena did this to me in the eye-tower,' she said.

Morpeth examined her hand. 'It's nothing. Just a cut.'

'It's not just a cut,' Rachel said firmly. 'Dragwena said it would transform me into a Witch. She said I'd start to look like her.'

'How many mouths has Dragwena got?' asked Morpeth.

'Four.'

'And what about her skin? Are there any freckles on her nose?'

Rachel half-smiled. 'No, of course not.'

'In that case stop worrying. I see one mouth, and your

freckles are as bold as ever. Nothing about you is different. Let's go.'

He took her other hand and they set off on their snowshoes across the frozen waters of Lake Ker.

Rachel and Morpeth made their way steadily across the ice. As usual the sun shone weakly in the sky, barely piercing the high grey clouds.

'Tell me about the wolves,' Rachel said, as she struggled to keep up with him.

'They are Dragwena's special pets,' Morpeth explained. 'They were ordinary dogs once. Over the years the Witch fashioned them in her own way: made them larger, gave them snouts which can pick up the tiniest scent. Unlike most animals on this world wolves can *speak*. In the past I have been responsible for their training. They are intelligent and ruthless creatures, and every last one does the bidding of Dragwena.'

'Are there any near us?'

'Wolves are never far away.'

Rachel gazed nervously around, expecting huge paw tracks to be criss-crossing the snow. But there were no signs of wolves. The snows stretched out confidently, as if daring anything alive to disturb their featureless grey. Nothing moved or stirred. Even the pallid sky was empty. So quiet, Rachel thought. Was that good or bad? She cleared the snow of Lake Ker beneath her feet, wondering if bright fish might be shivering under the lake's surface, but there was just the impenetrable blackness of ice forever frozen.

'What's down there?' she asked.

'Nothing,' said Morpeth. 'Unless it can live without breathing. Unless it can live without moving or eating. Perhaps Dragwena has created such a creature, just to know that it suffers. Come on, we can't rest here.'

'But what other creatures live on Ithrea?' Rachel asked, staying close to him. 'I've seen so few.'

'Eagles live in the western mountains, helping the Sarren where they can,' he said. 'They only survive because Dragwena likes to keep a few alive, to hunt when she's bored. The wolves devour anything that lives on the surface. The only other animals live underground – if you can call them animals. Who knows what they might have been once, but most are now weak slug-like creatures, blind, slurping what scraps they can find from the deep earth. Even Dragwena can't be bothered to torment them.'

Rachel heard a tiny flutter. It was a pair of birds, streaking across the sky. They flew in perfect formation, their movements incredibly precise.

Morpeth pulled her down. 'Keep dead still,' he hissed.

'What are they?'

'Prapsies,' he said. 'Dragwena's spies. Half-bird, half-baby, and much faster than eagles.'

'Half baby?' Rachel whispered.

'They're weird, mixed-up things,' Morpeth said. 'Joke-creations of the Witch. Don't ask me to describe them. You wouldn't believe me.'

The prapsies zigzagged in several directions across the sky. They travelled in exact straight lines, occasionally stopping and hovering, without needing to slow down. At one point they passed over Rachel and Morpeth and she heard them chattering loudly – a babble of high-pitched voices.

Morpeth waited several minutes before continuing, and now they moved more cautiously. After walking for over an hour they crossed Lake Ker and headed towards the low hills. To Rachel the hills seemed miles away, and the murky wood even further. She noticed her hand throbbing painfully and glanced down.

'Morpeth!' she cried.

Where the puncture wound had stood a clear black circle now lay etched on her palm; inside the circle was a perfect five-pointed star. Rachel knew where she had seen that shape before – on the candle in the eye-tower.

'What's this?' she asked, looking squarely at Morpeth. 'It's some kind of Witch-mark, isn't it?'

'Yes,' he admitted.

'Does it mean I'm changing into a Witch?'

'You still don't look like Dragwena, if that is what you mean. Do you feel any different?'

'No, I don't . . . think so,' said Rachel. 'But this mark has grown in a few hours. If it's a Witch-mark Dragwena must have done something to me. I'm scared, Morpeth.'

'It's probably nothing,' he said, trying to draw her on.

'You don't know what it means, do you?' she said, standing her ground. 'What if it means I'll be a Witch by the time I reach Latnap Deep? Eric's there. I don't want to harm him, or anyone else.'

Morpeth regarded her gravely. 'I don't know what the mark signifies. No Sarren has ever had this mark. It could mean *anything*. Your first thought is for Eric's safety. That tells me you are still the Rachel I know. We must trust in that.'

They shuffled on, their snowshoes carving through the

snows. Morpeth kept up a fast pace and Rachel, thinking of Dragwena, did not complain. But after several hours of trudging through the everlasting cold she entered a state of exhaustion, her whole body numb with pain and weariness.

Morpeth chatted constantly, trying to keep her alert. Eventually they arrived at the low hills. Rachel was too weary to notice or care. Morpeth let her rest and made his way to the top of a small rise.

Due south lay the safety of Latnap Deep, so close now. Between them and it stood the trees of Dragwood. Which way to go? Dragwood was dangerous, full of Dragwena's magic, easily stirred. They could go around Dragwood, but that would take over an hour, and Morpeth sensed the detour was beyond Rachel. Not once had she mentioned her tiredness, or complained, but Morpeth saw her fatigue in every step – and he was too weary himself to carry her all the way to Latnap Deep.

He glanced at the sky. A bleak sunset had set in, casting deep shadows around the trees. Soon it would be dark and unendurably cold. Even with her furs, Morpeth knew, Rachel would not survive a night on the surface. Making up his mind, he trotted back and found her lying on her side, half-buried by snow.

'Wake up, sleepyhead,' he murmured, lifting her up. 'It's not time for bed yet. We're going to take a short cut through the wood. We'll be in Latnap Deep within the hour.'

The last rays of the sun vanished. Above them, a few lonely stars and the great moon Armath shone brightly. Morpeth prayed Armath would shine well – its cold radiance was their only hope to pass swiftly through the trees: there were no footpaths in Dragwood.

'Stay close,' Morpeth said, linking hands with Rachel, and stepping more boldly than he felt into the outer trees.

14

PRAPSIES

As soon as Rachel and Morpeth crept inside Dragwood towering trees enfolded them in near darkness. A few moonbeams sliced between the upper branches, stabbing the ground with a piercing brilliance. Rachel listened anxiously to the tremor of a light wind. It rippled through the treetops, causing the branches to creak like doors opening.

At first they made rapid progress. As they penetrated further into Dragwood the trees packed together, their high, gnarled roots making it harder to stay on a straight course. They stumbled along as best they could, Rachel always clutching tightly onto Morpeth.

Then Morpeth squeezed her hand.

'What's wrong?' she asked.

He winced as Rachel's voice rang in the air.

'Listen,' he whispered.

Rachel held her breath. 'I can't hear anything.'

'Exactly. There is a breeze but the leaves on the trees are no longer rustling. Nothing's moving. Look!'

He pointed at the canopy of the wood.

On every tree the leaves pointed stiffly, like outstretched fingers. The branches had also stopped swaying, as if stilled to listen. Morpeth and Rachel staggered warily on.

Then, without warning, a branch lashed at Rachel's head. Other trees also started to shake, thrashing their leaves, warning the trees ahead about the strangers.

'What's happening?' Rachel squealed.

'Dragwood has awakened!' replied Morpeth.

And they ran for their lives.

They ducked under the lowest branches, tearing through the leaves, tripping and falling, picking each other up and running on. Ahead, Rachel suddenly noticed a spot where the trunks thinned slightly – an opening to the edge of the wood. They dashed towards the gap.

As they neared it two huge branches reached over their heads, ripping off their white cloaks. Instantly, as if a million eyes had been opened, all the leaves in Dragwood lashed the air. Several nearby trunks swayed. They snapped their roots, pulling themselves out of the ground.

'They can't run after us, can they?' screamed Rachel.

'They don't need to,' said Morpeth.

Rachel watched as the uprooted trees were passed from branch to branch of other trunks, until six of them were slammed into the earth, encircling Morpeth and Rachel.

There was no way through the trees. Dragwood, now fully awakened, had no intention of letting them escape.

For a moment Rachel and Morpeth stood in silence amidst the trunks, while leaves showered them from above, and Dragwood decided what to do.

At last, two of the largest trees dragged their slashed roots forward and felt with their branches for Morpeth's throat.

'Wait!' snapped a voice behind him.

The trees froze instantly. Even Morpeth froze because he recognized the voice behind him at once: Dragwena.

He turned to see Rachel standing with her head proudly erect, hands on hips, addressing the trees.

'Do you not recognize me?' she purred, her voice so perfectly like the Witch that no one except Dragwena herself would have been able to tell the difference. Rachel reached into her pocket and thrust her knife against Morpeth's neck. 'Let me through with this creature,' she commanded.

She did not wait for the trees to react. She walked confidently forward, dragging Morpeth with her. Slowly, uncertainly, the trees parted and allowed them through, their branches whispering. She pointed imperiously at the last tree blocking her path and it scuttled aside.

Rachel and Morpeth walked quickly to the edge of Dragwood, Rachel holding the knife against his throat all the way.

'Keep walking – don't run,' warned Morpeth.

Twenty footsteps took them safely out of reach of the trees. Rachel released Morpeth and stuffed the knife back into her jacket. Immediately the trees realized they had been tricked. They crowded at the edge of the wood, whipping their branches.

Rachel eyed them anxiously, ready to run. 'Why don't they come after us?'

'It seems they cannot leave Dragwood,' said Morpeth. 'Their magic must be confined to its limits.' He grinned, then stiffened.

'What is it?' Rachel asked.

'Quiet!' Morpeth hissed. 'Stay still!'

Behind them, peering from the outer trees of Dragwood, were two flying creatures with human faces.

Each had the black body of a crow, but on its neck perched a small human head: a pink face, snub nose, tiny round ears and soft thin hair – the face of a *baby*. They were so bizarre that Rachel would have burst out laughing had Morpeth not looked so concerned.

'Mine,' said one of the creatures, its voice high-pitched and baby-like too.

'No, mine,' said the other. 'I saw it first.'

'I saw the trees moving.'

'I saw it first!'

'You would not have seen it if I had not seen the trees.'

Its companion stuck out a tongue and blew a raspberry. The other spat at it.

'Missed me.'

'Meant to miss you.'

Together they turned their heads towards Rachel and Morpeth.

'What are they?' one asked.

'A man and a girl.'

'They do not move. Men and girls move. These do not. Therefore, they are something else.'

'A puzzle. Let's have a closer look.'

'After you.'

'After *you*,' chirped the other, bowing – and they both glided down together. One perched itself on Rachel's head; the other landed on Morpeth's shoulder. Rachel tried not to blink. The one on her head bent down and pressed the tip of its tiny pink tongue against her cheek.

'Soft skin,' it said. 'Must be girl. Tastes nice.'

The other child-bird bit Morpeth on the ear. Rachel saw him tense, stifling a cry.

'Frozen man. Statue. Not real.'

'But I saw it move.'

'It does not move.'

'It moved! I saw it!'

'Rubbish!'

'You're rubbish!'

'You're rubbish!'

The child-birds argued like this for some time, while Morpeth and Rachel remained as still as they could.

'Let's go away and watch them,' suggested one of the child-birds, eventually.

The other scratched its ear with a claw. 'Agreed. After you.'

'After *you*,' said its companion, bowing – and they both flew off together. Each retook its original position in the trees and perched there, quietly twitching and staring at Rachel and Morpeth from a short distance.

'Prapsies?' whispered Rachel, trying to stay motion-less.

'Yes,' said Morpeth. 'Probably the same pair we saw earlier. They can't harm us, but nothing flies more swiftly. They could warn Dragwena of our presence. Don't move.

They are stupid creatures and quickly become bored. If we stay still they may just fly away.'

Several times the prapsies flew down and landed on or near them, then flitted back to the trees, continually arguing amongst themselves.

'Statues. Definitely statues.'

'Yes,' said the other. 'Warm statues.'

'Will we tell Dragwena?'

'No. Silly mistake. She will spank us if we tell her about statues.'

They giggled.

'Let's go then.'

'After you.'

'After *you*,' said the other, bowing – and together they sprang from the tree. But at that moment Rachel felt a cramp in her right leg and had to lift it from the ground. The prapsies immediately hovered, chattering wildly.

'Real child and man. Alive! Alive!'

'Pretend statues! Man and girl.'

'Rachel and Morpeth!'

'Morpeth and Rachel!'

'Tell Dragwena at once.'

'At once.' Somehow, while flying in circles, they managed to bow to each other. 'After you,' they said – and flew off together.

Morpeth hurled a stick, but they easily dodged aside.

'Tell Dragwena!' squeaked one child-bird.

'Tell Dragwena and the wolves!'

'Tell the wolves!'

'Tell the wolves!'

'Eat them up—'

'For supper!'

The prapsies sped off, heading northwards, muttering 'wolves, wolves, wolves!' in glee until they were out of sight.

15

WOLVES

Morpeth watched the flight path the child-birds had taken.

'They're heading for Dragwena in the Ragged Mountains,' he said. 'The journey is short for a prapsy. Now we have a race to beat the Witch to Latnap Deep.'

Rachel shivered. With the onset of night snow had started falling heavily, bringing with it a searing wind. Behind them the trees of Dragwood continued their urgent, relentless thrashing.

'Morpeth, I can't go much further,' she said. 'Can't we hide?'

'There is nowhere to hide on the surface from the Witch,' Morpeth said, gripping her tightly. 'We *can* get to Latnap Deep! It's not too far. Please – I know how tired you are. Make one last effort.'

Rachel nodded weakly, barely able to force a smile any longer.

Despite the danger they set off at an agonizingly slow pace. It was all Rachel could manage, and they had also lost their snowshoes in Dragwood, making every footfall heavy through the snow. They skirted Dragwood, heading westwards for a time through the slush of boggy land.

Eventually they turned south again. Ahead, a wide undulating moor rose gently before them, and normally Rachel would not even have noticed the effort of walking across. But her last reserves of strength had vanished in the slush, and she moved through a numbing exhaustion. Only fear of the Witch kept her dead feet moving. She planted one reluctant step in front of the other, too tired to think ahead.

Morpeth allowed Rachel to lean against his shoulder, protecting her face as best he could from the buffeting of the wind. They seemed to walk forever like this, freezing gusts piercing their clothes and Armath so bright that without their cloaks they were lit up for all to see in the snow.

At last Morpeth permitted Rachel another rest. He knew Dragwena would soon arrive – their clumsy footsteps would be like blazing beacons to her night vision and the wolves. Rachel slept, her face already half-buried by dark snow. Morpeth heaved her over his back. He lowered his face and walked steadily into the brunt of the wind, sheer desperation carrying his legs.

Then he noticed the wolf.

It was eight feet high from paw to shoulder. Thirty or more of the beasts had surrounded them without him noticing. Icy breath steamed around their muzzles, and their glistening yellow eyes gazed in an almost leisurely way at Morpeth and Rachel. The leader of the wolves casually trotted forward. It was Scorpa, a she-wolf:

ferocious, sleek and deadly. Morpeth knew her well, as he had trained her as a cub.

'Hello, old man,' Scorpa said. 'I see Rachel has made you handsome. It's a pity she forgot to change the way you *smell*. That was a mistake.'

The wolf pack grinned.

Morpeth roused Rachel. He had to shake her several times.

'Welcome, child,' said Scorpa, bowing courteously. 'To greet one who has escaped Dragwena herself is a rare honour.'

'Leave us!' Rachel tried weakly, using Dragwena's voice.

Most of the wolves stirred uneasily. Scorpa simply rocked back on her grizzled hindquarters and howled with derision. 'Not a bad try. But we are not so easily fooled as the trees of Dragwood.'

Morpeth held his knife against Rachel's throat.

'Leave us or I will kill her!' he growled.

A wolf darted in, plucking the blade from his hand.

'Not fast enough,' tutted Scorpa. 'Rachel has given you a lean young body, but it moves like a geriatric. Another mistake. Still, Dragwena will soon polish the child's rough edges.' She licked her lips, pawing the ground. 'I give you a choice, Morpeth: I can set the pack on you at once – or you can do me the honour of single combat. I promise the others will not interfere. At least you will have a chance to tickle my flesh before you die. What do you say?'

The other wolves moved back slightly, giving them space.

Morpeth abruptly raised his hands. A blue light shot from them, piercing the sky like a flare.

'Do you hope for rescue even now?' Scorpa scoffed. 'Come. I grow weary. Choose!'

Morpeth spat at her muzzle.

'I choose to fight!'

He moved into the combat circle. The wolf with the knife tossed the blade back and he gripped it in his right hand, close against his hip, warrior fashion. With his left hand he beckoned Scorpa towards him.

'Come on, then!' he roared. 'Or are you *afraid*, she-wolf?'

Scorpa bared her fangs and they slowly circled each other, probing for weaknesses. The wolf padded deftly and, when she pounced, there was no warning – her movement so swift that Rachel hardly saw it. Scorpa sunk her jaw into his thigh, then jumped aside. Morpeth stifled a scream but stayed on his feet – to fall would mean instant death. Scorpa pounced again. Feigning to attack the same leg, she changed direction at the last moment and caught Morpeth turning. Even as he realized his mistake her fangs ripped through his stomach, and when she raised her muzzle it dripped with blood and torn flesh. Scorpa leapt away at once, and Morpeth's weak slash at her underbelly missed.

'You have become feeble, old man,' gloated Scorpa, 'while I have grown strong. I am not the cub you bested long ago. I hoped for a better fight than this.'

Morpeth tottered in the circle, facing her again.

'An enemy is always at its most dangerous when it is desperate,' he growled. 'I taught you that, remember. Your strength never matched my cunning.'

But his words sounded hollow and Scorpa knew it.

'Time to finish you off,' she said, aiming for his throat.

She never reached him. As Scorpa leapt a huge white eagle, as large as the wolf itself, swooped out of the darkness, sinking its talons into her neck. At the same instant two other eagles dropped down, grasped Rachel and Morpeth and shot into the air. The wolves snapped at their tails, but the fangs fell short and the birds made their escape, carrying Morpeth and Rachel upwards into the cloud. Within seconds they left the wolves baying far behind and were heading south.

'Latnap Deep!' Morpeth urged, wincing with the pain of his injuries. 'Take us to the Deep, Ronnocoden!'

The great white eagle bent his head towards Morpeth to obtain the exact directions. With the onset of night he had circled with his companions within the safety of the low snow clouds, waiting for any signal. Now the great birds cut purposefully through the storm. Within swift, almost silent, wingbeats Morpeth and Rachel were carried through the sky, the eagles dropping out of the cloud at the last possible moment to avoid detection.

Morpeth fell from the back of Ronnocoden and pounded his fists into the featureless snow. Six times. Four times. Three times. A few feet away the snow collapsed over a secret door, and avid arms pulled them inside. The eagles instantly took flight southwards.

Rachel blinked in the bright light of the tunnel before them. Three Sarren stood there and, a little to one side, Trimak gasped at the blood pouring through Morpeth's jacket.

Trimak worked furiously to stem Morpeth's bleeding.

Scorpa had performed her task well: the stomach was torn open and Morpeth's life-blood pumped from the wound, spreading thickly.

Trimak knew how to repair broken bones, minor burns or light bleeding, but this – this was an injury beyond his abilities. Morpeth's grey face was already creased with the effort to remain conscious.

In a few minutes, Trimak knew, Morpeth would be dead.

Morpeth also knew. He looked at his ripped stomach and weakly lifted his head.

'Well,' he said, with a faint smile. 'I think this wound is beyond even your skilful hands, my old friend. I should have allowed Ronnocoden to carry us all the way here from the Palace, but feared the Witch would expect help from that direction. I made the wrong choice, travelling on foot. I have made so many mistakes . . . so many.'

'Heal yourself!' Trimak ordered. 'You have come too far to leave us now.'

Morpeth's face writhed in pain. 'Heal myself? I think even if my powers were at their full I could not repair this injury. And I have nothing left. Nothing.'

Trimak cast his face down to conceal his emotions. 'You brought back the child-hope!' he said. 'Against impossible odds you rescued her twice. There is still hope for us, thanks to you.'

'Guard her well,' Morpeth said. 'Rachel is so weary. Let her rest.'

'Always thinking of others,' said Trimak. He looked away, tears splashing down his cheeks.

'At least Dragwena will never touch me now,' murmured Morpeth. 'I have denied her that, at any rate.'

His body slumped against the tunnel wall and his bright blue eyes closed.

Trimak buried his face in Morpeth's shoulder, weeping with abandon, tears bursting from him.

Rachel staggered across to Morpeth. 'Don't give up!' she shouted at Trimak. 'What's wrong with you? Make him live! Do something!'

Trimak stared uselessly at the floor. Rachel put her hands on the blood pouring from Morpeth, trying to hold it in.

Morpeth was not dead, not quite. He managed to open his eyes. 'Rachel, nothing is wrong which you cannot right.' He looked sternly at her. 'It is up to you now.'

'Don't die!' Rachel pleaded. 'Don't die, Morpeth. I can't bear it!'

'You must,' he said.

His head sunk heavily into the hands of Trimak.

All the Sarren bent on one knee and raised their swords.

'No! No! No!' Rachel screamed. 'I won't let you die. I won't!'

She pushed Trimak off and gripped Morpeth's cheeks. He was still breathing slightly, shallowly. Rachel forced his eyes open and stared into them. What could she do? *There must be something!* She felt her mind tug – and looked down: where before there had only been a mess of bone and blood, Rachel suddenly saw the way to heal Morpeth laid out like a diagram. She did not wait to ponder how this could be. Precisely, like a scalpel, her mind sought the wound, the blood, each torn muscle, the veins, the epidermal layers. She acted immediately.

Beneath her Morpeth convulsed and lifted his head. His stomach moved beneath the muscles. Layers of new flesh grew from the tatters, sealing the wound. A new belly-button appeared with a *pop* where the old one had been torn off.

All the Sarren gazed in disbelief at Rachel.

'How did you do this?' Morpeth gasped.

'I – I don't know,' Rachel said honestly. She searched her mind for the source of her new powers, sensing a different layer of magic growing inside, more powerful, itching to be used. But as she explored for answers a wave of exhaustion swept her. Now Morpeth was safe she could barely keep her eyes open. 'I'm so tired . . .' she mumbled. 'Too . . . tired to think.'

'Then sleep,' Morpeth said. 'No one deserves it more than you.' He laughed, and his voice rang with life. 'Sleep, and when you wake up we'll have breakfast together again!'

'I want to see Eric,' Rachel said weakly.

'He is being well cared for.'

'I'm scared about the dreams I might have, Morpeth. Please. I don't want to go to sleep.'

'Have happy dreams,' he said. 'Dragwena is far away now. She cannot harm you. I won't allow her to get close. I promise.'

Rachel sat on Morpeth's lap, leant against his shoulder and fell asleep at once, too weary even to explore her new gifts and what they meant.

16

Latnap Deep

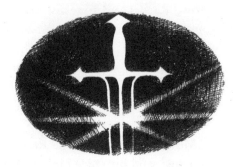

Rachel slept through the night and late into the afternoon of the next day. Ithrea's sun had begun its bleak sunset, spreading watery whites across the sky, when she finally awoke. She was in a soft bed which Morpeth had himself prepared. He lay slumped in a chair a few feet away, snoring gently.

Rachel crept quietly out of bed, careful not to wake Morpeth, and washed herself using a bowl left for her in the room. Fresh garments had been placed beside the bed: rough woollen pants and a thick brown linen shirt. They were not the magnificent clothes she could have chosen from her wardrobe in the Palace, but they fitted well enough and Rachel now preferred them.

She sat on the edge of the bed and coughed loudly.

Morpeth grunted and looked up with his bright blue eyes.

'Hello, handsome,' Rachel smiled. 'Am I too late for breakfast?'

Morpeth stretched and eyed her. 'Of course not! But we do not have as much choice here as the Breakfast Room at the Palace.'

'It doesn't matter. Anything will do.'

He patted his stomach. 'Lovely belly-button,' he said. 'An improvement on my old one. Much neater.'

'I don't know how I did it,' said Rachel, seriously. 'What does it mean? I know my magic's been developing quickly, but not that fast.'

'I've no idea,' he admitted. 'But I'm grateful. Look at me – handsome, supremely fit, a match for any Neutrana soldier!' He jumped four feet in the air, turned a perfect somersault and landed on his toes. 'I don't know what you did, Rachel, but I feel fantastic!'

'How is Eric?' asked Rachel.

'Ah! You may well ask. I think you'd better come and see the amazing Eric for yourself. You won't believe what he's up to. Come on.'

Morpeth linked their arms and escorted her to a room where Eric sat on a small chair. Rachel burst into tears, holding him tightly for several seconds, not wanting to let go.

'Hey, are you all right?' she asked at last, smoothing out his hair.

'I'm OK.' He laughed. 'Better look out! I can do things now. *Special* things. Tell her, Morpeth.'

Morpeth grinned. 'Remember our games in the Breakfast Room?'

'Of course,' she said.

'Pick something to imagine. Anything.'

Rachel shrugged. 'A flower?'

'Very well. Now watch.'

A moment later a daffodil floated in the air above Morpeth's head.

Eric poked his finger at the flower. It disappeared.

Morpeth created six different bunches of flowers and made them race around the ceiling.

Eric zapped them with his wand-like finger, one by one.

'He's got magic!' Rachel cried. 'He can do the things we can do!'

'No, you're wrong,' said Morpeth. He glanced at Eric. 'Make a bunch of flowers.'

'I can't,' Eric said. 'You know that.'

'Try again,' Morpeth urged him. 'Go on.'

Eric screwed up his face for several seconds, lips pressed hard together. Finally, with an irritated groan, he gave up. 'I can't do it. So what. Everyone's got magic here. That's nothing special.'

'I don't understand,' said Rachel. 'What power has Eric got?'

'I'm not sure,' said Morpeth. 'A very unusual power, certainly. I've never seen it before in any child brought to Ithrea. I think I would describe it as *anti-magic*. Eric makes magic disappear.'

Rachel frowned. 'I can do that, too. In the Breakfast Room we both made things disappear.'

'Not in the same way as Eric,' Morpeth said. 'See for yourself. Create something.'

Rachel made a single object, a replica of the perfectly built oak table her granddad had crafted shortly before he died last winter. It was an object she knew well, as he had shown her lovingly how he had made every detail – the joints, the secret drawer, the many layers of varnish, all patiently applied. Rachel took her time, forming the table carefully and then placed the image in the centre of the room.

Eric, without even looking at it, pointed. Instantly the table vanished. Rachel tried to rebuild it, but found that she could no longer remember clearly what it looked like. She concentrated furiously, but could only remake a table that looked slightly like the original.

Eventually, she stared in amazement at Eric.

'Try something else,' said Morpeth.

So Rachel made a lamp instead, focusing hard. That disappeared too, and again she could no longer recreate it.

'Now do you see!' Morpeth cried. 'Eric takes away magic *permanently!* Whatever you can create he can destroy, and it seems to be impossible to use that same spell again. It has gone *forever.'*

Rachel immediately thought of Dragwena. 'Can you destroy the Witch's magic, too?'

'Maybe. I'm not sure,' said Eric hesitantly. 'Some of it. Not her best magic. She can hide things. And I think Dragwena's got some magic that's lots of spells together, changing all the time. They could mix me up.'

'Why didn't you do any of this before?' Rachel asked.

'I didn't know I could,' he said. 'It did it by accident. Morpeth was practising his magic. He was annoying me. I wanted it to stop and – swish!'

Rachel pinched his nose, wondering what to say. 'You're . . . I can't do anything like this!'

Eric beamed happily. It was the first time Rachel had seen him look his old cocky self since arriving on Ithrea. I wonder, she thought. For a moment she pictured herself fighting Dragwena while Eric waved his anti-magic finger, undoing the Witch's spells one by one.

She sat down at a large stone table and made a fuss over Eric until Morpeth brought her a bowl of soup and a chunk of rough bread.

'No chocolate sandwiches, I'm afraid,' he apologized.

While she ate Eric edged closer to Rachel, looking closely at her hair.

'Ugh!' he said, pulling away. 'It's grey. Your hair's all grey.'

Rachel lifted her fringe. Her scalp felt dry and flaky. She dashed to a nearby mirror and parted her hair in several places. Everywhere, under the surface, it was white and thin. She yanked and a tuft filled her hand.

'What's the matter with me, Morpeth?' she asked in shock. 'Am I – am I growing *old* like you and Trimak because I've been using too much magic?'

Morpeth touched the strands. 'It's probably nothing,' he replied lightly. 'The stress of recent events. Using magic doesn't change you that quickly.'

Rachel continued to gaze in the mirror, trying to see if she had the typical wrinkles of the Sarren around her eyes. There were no wrinkles but there were *other* changes – her jaw felt tender and her eyes ached.

As she pondered this Trimak appeared in the doorway. He looked exhausted. 'Do you want to look around Latnap Deep, Rachel?' he asked. 'It's not . . . a pretty sight, I'm afraid.'

Rachel held Eric's hand, still rubbing her sore eyes, and entered the main caves.

They were full of injured Sarren. Small makeshift beds, little more than rags of clothing, covered the floor and dozens of men and women lay still or softly moaning. A few of the least wounded moved between them, administering simple medicines and offering comfort as best they could.

Rachel stared at the Sarren, appalled. 'What happened?'

'They fought the Neutrana under the Palace,' Trimak said. 'Most had only their hands as weapons. Only a hundred or so are left. The rest died in the tunnels, or on the journey to Latnap Deep.'

'You *walked*?' marvelled Rachel. 'You mean, you came all that way in the snow without Dragwena finding you?'

'It was a terrible journey,' said Trimak. 'Fear of the Witch drove us through the blizzards. I believe we only made it because Dragwena's spies were searching for a bigger prize – they were looking for *you*.'

Rachel gazed numbly at the injured Sarren, and suddenly everything she had endured, everything they had all suffered since she and Eric arrived on Ithrea, seemed too much to bear.

'It's all our fault!' she said. 'Dragwena *let* me escape just to trap the Sarren together under the Palace. Then she used Eric to keep track of me. Perhaps she's still using both of us. Dragwena might be able to find you all in Latnap Deep because *we're* here. Did you think of that?'

'Yes. Of course,' said Trimak. 'It's a risk we must take.'

'Is it?' asked Rachel. 'I know you believe I'm the child-hope. You want me to fight Dragwena. I know I must do that. But—' she held back her tears, clutching Eric. 'But—'

'You're frightened of the Witch,' said Trimak. 'I know. We all are.' His eyes moistened, and he hung his head. 'We are asking so much of you.'

Rachel held her long hair, no longer completely dark, in both hands. 'I don't mind that,' she said. 'But have you seen this? Look, I'm no longer your dark-haired child any more, am I?' She stared at Morpeth. 'I will do anything to keep you and Eric safe, but what have I managed so far? I couldn't even frighten a few wolves. Eric points his little finger and my spells are gone, just like that. How do you expect me to defeat the Witch? You have no idea how powerful she is. I think Dragwena might just be playing with us. She flies around and amuses herself by killing Sarren and stroking her disgusting snake. What can I really do to frighten her?'

For a moment there was a tense silence in the cave. Then Rachel noticed a man kneeling down a short distance away – a man Rachel recognized: Grimwold. 'I remember you,' she said. 'You gave me a chance to escape from the eye-tower.'

Grimwold's face was badly cut. One of his ears had been torn off.

'The child-hope,' he gasped. 'Then all those deaths . . . were not in vain.' He reached out, gripping Rachel's arm. 'Are you really the child-hope? Are you? How many more deaths must there be?'

Rachel read Grimwold's expression – his despair and

hope. 'Oh, that stupid verse,' she muttered. 'I don't know what it means. What use is it? I can't even *remember* it clearly.'

Grimwold kept his grip on her arm, and said:

> *'Dark girl she will be,*
> *Enemies to set free,*
> *Sing in harmony,*
> *From sleep and dawn-bright sea,*
> *I will arise,*
> *And behold your childish glee.'*

'It still doesn't mean anything to me,' said Rachel.

'I know another verse,' Eric whispered.

Everyone froze.

'A dark verse,' he said.

Rachel glanced at Trimak. 'Do you know what he means?'

All the Sarren shook their heads fearfully.

Eric cleared his throat, and said:

> *'Dark girl she will be,*
> *Fair hearts broken,*
> *Ancient wrath awoken,*
> *Children unborn,*
> *Wizards under lawn,*
> *Darkness without dawn.'*

As Eric finished all the Sarren covered their ears, howling with pain.

'What does it mean?' Rachel asked, bewildered.

'It means this,' Eric said under his breath. '*Fair hearts broken, children unborn, Wizards under lawn, darkness without dawn*. Dragwena's going to kill all the children and the Wizards, just like she told Rachel.'

'Why didn't you tell us this before?' said Rachel. 'Something this important—'

'I didn't know the words, until just now,' Eric protested feebly. 'Don't ask me why!'

'It's me, isn't it?' Rachel said. 'Dragwena needs *me* to fulfil the dark verse. She needs my power. And if she turns me into a Witch I'll help her do all these terrible things. I am the child-hope or . . . the *end* of all hope.'

Morpeth and Trimak looked at the floor, unable to meet Rachel's gaze.

'You don't know *anything*, do you?' she said, hardly able to contain her frustration. 'You expect me to know! Are we just going to wait for Dragwena to come and get us? I'm sick of it, hiding and running away. There must be something we can do. How long will it take Dragwena to find us?'

'Weeks perhaps,' Trimak said. 'Days more likely. The Witch may already know we are here.'

Rachel pulled Eric towards her. 'What are we going to do?'

Eric started to cry, big tears tumbling down his cheeks. 'Rachel, I don't know. You'll think of something. The Witch hasn't got you yet.'

And then Rachel heard someone laugh.

The voice was not human. Rachel recognized it instantly: Dragwena.

17

teeth

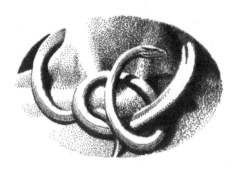

Rachel glanced wildly round the cave.

'*I am not in this dingy pit,*' Dragwena's voice scoffed.

Rachel thought, 'Then – where?'

'*Within you, child.*'

A thumping terror shuddered through Rachel. 'H-how can you be?'

'*Look at your hand.*'

Rachel opened her fingers. The five-pointed star of the Witch-mark, now thickly black, blazed on her palm.

'*I am finishing the task interrupted by the Sarren in the eye-tower,*' Dragwena explained. '*The wound I gave you then went deep. The transformation to Witch will be painless and swift now. Already your blood is thinning, altering in colour. Finally it will be vibrant emerald, too bright for your human eyes to bear. But by then your eyes will no longer be human, either . . .*'

Rachel tore at the Witch-mark with her nails. The blood

that poured out was yellow. Her mind shrieked: 'What have you done to me? This can't be happening?'

'*Your friends in the caves will certainly get a shock,*' Dragwena laughed. '*They think you are the child-hope to guide them home. What a surprise they will get when four Witch jaws thrust from your face, crawling with spiders.*'

Rachel felt her mouth. She noticed a solid hard mass burgeoning under the flesh of both cheeks.

'*In a few hours the change will be complete,*' Dragwena told her. '*You will no longer need sleep. Your eyelids will dissolve. Your nostrils will split and fold into sensitive flaps of skin, revealing extraordinary new scents. You will enjoy all this, I promise.*'

Rachel closed her eyes tightly, desperate to block out the voice.

'*That will not work,*' Dragwena said. '*I can now read your every thought, know your fears and hopes. There can be no escape. Do not struggle. Give yourself up to me willingly.*'

Rachel's entire body convulsed with fear. She gazed desperately around for help, stumbled and fell on the cave floor.

'Rachel, what is it?' said Morpeth, rushing to pick her up.

Eric walked across the room and did something he had not done since he had been little more than a baby – he put his arms around Rachel's neck. He squeezed her tightly, and Rachel sobbed into his embrace, wave on bursting wave of tears.

'I *know*,' he whispered. 'Dragwena's inside you, isn't she?'

Rachel buried herself in his shoulder, too despondent to answer.

Morpeth stared at Eric. 'How do you know what is happening? How can you possibly know?'

'I just know. Rachel needs to be alone.'

Morpeth lifted Rachel and carried her from the cave to a small chamber where there was some privacy. Eric held her hand tightly all the way, encouraging her with bright little smiles, not in the least embarrassed. Rachel knew Eric never normally behaved like this. Did it mean she could no longer survive without his help?

Morpeth placed her gently on the floor, wiping away her tears. 'There,' he murmured, lifting her chin. 'We are alone, you and I and Eric.'

'Not alone,' she said. 'Dragwena is in me. She knows *everything* I know.'

'What should we do?' Morpeth asked. He asked Rachel, but he also turned to Eric, and it was Eric who answered.

'I'm not sure,' said Eric, 'but I think that if the Witch can get inside her head, then Rachel might be able to get inside Dragwena too.' He gripped Rachel's shoulders. 'Try, Rachel. Go on. Find out things about the Witch.'

Rachel nodded bleakly. Clutching Eric's hand she made herself relax. She closed her eyes, clearing her mind. And then slowly, hesitantly, with the utmost care, she began to probe. She reached down until she touched another presence – a presence burning with its own ancient, ancient desires: Dragwena.

'*Look long and well,*' Dragwena whispered. '*I have yearned for this moment, child. I would have preferred to have caught you before you reached Latnap Deep, but that is no longer important. It is so long since I could openly read another's thoughts like this. Only Witches have this gift. We began to talk this way in the eye-tower. Now it is much easier. So you see we will soon be Witches together. I need have no secrets from you now. Look further.'*

Dragwena's mind spread wide in invitation, and Rachel streaked through the dark secrets of her memory. She experienced sensations that brought Dragwena comfort – the caress of her soul-snake; the joy of riding within a storm-whirl at the edge of the world, the spiders hiding within the safety of her throat. And wolves. Rachel felt what it was like for Dragwena to be amongst the pack: the smell of wolves together on the hunt, and the Witch belly-close beside them, running everywhere and nowhere, following the chase wherever it led.

'*Go deeper,*' Dragwena urged.

Rachel did. She witnessed the Witch on a long search. Amongst the Ragged Mountains of Ithrea Dragwena flew as a bird, and beyond to the high poles, where the ice froze on her gigantic wings.

'What are you looking for?' asked Rachel.

'*For Larpskendya. The Wizard told me he would leave his song on this tiny world. I sought out the scent of his magic to kill his presence, wherever it hid.*'

Rachel watched as Dragwena changed into dozens of creatures. As a shark under the vast Endellion Ocean the Witch sought, her body diving deep to the rocky bed, where her mouth became a limitless maw grinding through a million sea-creatures with fluorescent gills. For centuries she searched. The Witch scoured in every corner of the world, and beneath the world, and in the high skies, by day and night, until Rachel had seen the alien constellations flash by so often that she knew them intimately.

At last Dragwena's search ended.

'You never found him,' Rachel realized. 'You don't even know what Larpskendya's song is. But it's still here, somewhere, isn't it? Protecting Ithrea. Protecting *us*.' Her heart soared. 'I remember the dream-sleep,' she said defiantly. 'Larpskendya promised to protect the children on Earth by developing their magic. He said they would be able to use it against you if needed.'

'No child has ever come with enough magic to challenge me,' said Dragwena. *'But Larpskendya kept his word. For long ages I have drawn children to Ithrea, and their powers are always improving. You are the strongest of all, Rachel. But you are not strong enough to defy me.'*

'I wonder,' Rachel said. Could she really be the child-hope? And Eric? What about his gift? Was it a threat to the Witch? She sensed fear in Dragwena's mind then, quickly masked, but fear nonetheless, and felt grateful. 'So, you couldn't find Larpskendya. Good. What did you do next, Witch?'

'This was his planet, Larpskendya's world. I hated everything. I changed it!'

Rachel watched the Witch skimming over the original bright forest world of Ithrea. When she touched the trees they blackened and died. Dragwena dragged her nails into the rich soils and the lush flowers withered. She blazed across the vibrant blue skies, turning them to lifeless grey, and the snow a deeper grey, and filtered the yellow light from the sun until all colour and warmth was removed utterly. Even that was not enough for the Witch. She reached into the deepest edges of the world and created the storm-whirls, belching lightning and cloud. Then Dragwena turned on the simple animals, giving crows the faces of babies and changing dogs into wolves the size of bears, who could talk and comfort her in her loneliness. And one day, on a whim, Rachel saw the Witch take forever the singing voices Larpskendya had given the eagles.

'I'm not surprised by anything you do now,' Rachel murmured. 'I've seen how you enjoy killing and maiming for no reason. I'll never let you use me to do that!'

Dragwena's voice laughed. '*We shall see. Eagles, children, everything you know or feel now will be meaningless soon. Only the battle with the Wizards is important, the endless war. But all is not war, Rachel. There is the Sisterhood of the Witches to bring warmth too. Would you like to see it? Would you like to see my home world, the planet of Ool – the Witchworld?*'

Rachel knew that Dragwena was trying to entice her. But this time, unlike the dream-sleep or her experiences in the eye-tower, Rachel felt that she could withstand the Witch. Confidently, she said, 'Show me your home world, then. It must be ugly, if you came from there.'

Rachel found herself floating above a gigantic planet. The sky was deep grey, almost black, and the lifeless sun offered no warmth. As Rachel expected, she saw the storm-whirls – but unlike Ithrea, the whirls on Ool covered the whole planet. And inside, riding the whirl-tops, Rachel saw the Witches, millions of them. They flew on the raging blasts, practising their spells. As Rachel watched she felt a yearning to be there, riding with the Witches. Who were they? What were their names? All were female. Mothers? Sisters? They beckoned, lifting up their bare arms, imploring Rachel to join them.

Rachel wanted to fly amongst the Witches. She knew this feeling, dragging her inside Dragwena's desires, and resisted it. She dismissed the Ool World from her mind, and knew that Dragwena had not expected this.

'How did you bring the children from Earth?' Rachel demanded.

Rachel now saw Dragwena sitting alone in the unending snows of Ithrea. *'Larpskendya made sure I could not leave the planet. I was trapped, but I began a spell, a single finding spell. It required a dozen years, Rachel, to initiate, and a hundred more to perfect, and the making of it almost destroyed me.'* Rachel watched the years of the spell's creation flash by. During it the Witch hardly changed from her position in the snow, barely moved even her head. The effort to finish the spell made Dragwena ill: her blood-red cheeks swarmed with maggots and her teeth rotted as the cleaning spiders died.

'Larpskendya made one mistake. He should never have told me he was developing magic on Earth. That gave me a faint hope. I put everything I had into creating this one spell. Finally it was complete.' Rachel stared as Dragwena dragged her sagging body to the top of the highest mountain of Ithrea, breathing at the radiant stars. The spell leapt through the sky. It pierced the outer world and spread in several directions, hunting.

'I waited a thousand years and longer,' Dragwena said, *'until I was so weakened I wondered if the wolves themselves might finish me off. But at last the spell found your Earth. And then I was able to draw children from it, bring them here and make use of their magic to revive me.'*

Rachel recalled the Wizards and the Child Army. 'Why didn't you return? You pledged to kill the children who turned against you. I know how much you hated them, still hate them.'

'*The magic of earlier children was not powerful enough. But I was patient and I waited. I knew one day a child would arrive strong enough to help me back – you, Rachel.*'

'I can read your mind as well as you can read mine,' said Rachel. 'It is dangerous for you to let me inside you, Witch. I'll discover a way to hurt you.'

Dragwena whispered, '*No, child, you do not understand. I intend to keep you here, linked to my mind, until I am sure the transformation is complete. When you are fully a Witch I will return you to the caves and let you loose. First, I think you should kill the betrayers, Morpeth and Trimak. After that we must decide how to use little Eric. Your brother has strengths I cannot yet fully understand. If we are unable to master them for our own purposes, we will destroy him. Perhaps I'll let you kill your own brother, Rachel – if the army I have sent does not reach Latnap Deep first.*'

Dragwena opened her mind, and Rachel saw Neutrana soldiers marching. Five thousand of them, armed for close fighting and flanked by wolves, headed steadily towards the caves of Latnap Deep. The army would arrive soon and Dragwena planned to kill everyone inside.

Everyone except Rachel.

'I'll warn them!' Rachel raged.

'*Try to get out. See if you can!*'

Rachel tugged her thoughts away, expecting to find herself back in the cave with Morpeth and Eric. Instead, she remained inside Dragwena's thoughts. She searched for the exit. There was none. The original route was blocked, or she had forgotten it. Every path she tried took her down, deeper into the Witch's mind.

'Let me go!'

Dragwena laughed, the sound filling Rachel's ears. *'The transformation is quickening. Sense it! Can't you feel the change? You already have new powers beyond anything Morpeth can conceive. You are becoming a Witch. Join me. Don't fight. It is pointless. Soon—'*

Suddenly: a blast.

Rachel felt it slam into her, like the shock-wave of a bomb. Then a further boom, twice as hard, followed by high-pitched screams: *Dragwena's* screams.

'What?' the Witch gasped.

Another explosion, and this time Rachel heard something tear. She looked up, and saw light gashing through the tear, and above the light a corner of Latnap Deep. Eric stood there, his face burning with concentration.

'Get out!' she heard Morpeth shout. 'Head towards us!'

'No!' said Eric. 'Look for spells first. Quickly, Rachel, find them. I'm opening up Dragwena for you.'

The blasts continued, ripping into Dragwena's mind, slicing it wide. Rachel did not hesitate. She spread her thoughts, ignoring Dragwena's agony. Rachel searched in the most secret regions, until she found what she was looking for: *spells* – delicate and powerful spells, changing spells, fast spells and spells of such complexity that they required unfathomable knowledge to summon. And, nestled deepest of all, were the death spells – a rich variety of death. Rachel touched them all, filling her mind.

Dragwena's shrieking ceased abruptly. Rachel blinked,

finding herself lying in the caves of Latnap Deep beside Eric and Morpeth.

Eric kicked the walls in frustration. 'What did you find?'

Rachel felt confused. 'I . . . don't . . . where is the Witch?'

'Gone! I kicked Dragwena out of your head. I smashed her magic. She ran. She *had* to run, back to the eye-tower!'

'H-how did you do that?'

Eric shook his head. 'I don't know how. I just attacked her magic. That's what I do, remember. I knew Dragwena was keeping you in there with her spells. I felt you trying to find a way out, so I reached in and killed the ones holding you there.' He grinned. 'Dragwena couldn't make them come back. Like you, she didn't know how!'

Rachel spent a few minutes considering what she had discovered. All the spells, including the death spells, remained in her mind. Was there something she could use to attack the Witch?

Her left cheek ached. Absently, she touched it – and immediately withdrew her hand.

Teeth, new teeth, were boiling under her skin.

She stared at Morpeth. *'What do I look like?'*

His face twisted.

'Tell me!'

Morpeth left the chamber briefly, returning with a mirror. Gripping it tightly, Rachel saw several things: her skin was red, blood-red; her nose a formless spongy mass. She examined her eyes. The lids were missing. She forced her lips open and noticed, embedded in the gums, three new sets of teeth. They were almost fully formed, white and backward curving, pushing at the flesh of her cheeks, ready to burst out.

Rachel dropped the mirror. She stood still, too terrified to cry out.

Morpeth gripped her shoulders. 'Yes, you are changing, but you are still the Rachel I know! Do you want to kill us? Do you?'

Rachel numbly shook her head.

'Then – we still have hope.'

'Hope?' Rachel replied angrily. 'Look at me! I'm *still* turning into a Witch! Dragwena told me this would happen.' She turned to Eric. 'How long before I completely change?'

'I don't know,' said Eric. 'I can't tell.'

'Can you get rid of it?' Rachel pleaded. 'It's a spell. It must be. Can't you stop what it's doing to me?'

Eric frowned. 'No. It is a spell, but somehow it's part of you, too. I can't work out what's happening. I don't know how to stop it.'

Rachel clenched her teeth. The new jaws meshed together perfectly.

'Take me to Trimak and the others,' she ordered Morpeth.

Back inside the main caves everyone gasped when they saw her. Several Sarren instinctively drew their swords. She quickly told them everything, including Dragwena's army approaching Latnap Deep.

Rachel noticed a man, obviously afraid, barely able to look up. She clacked her new jaws menacingly. 'You *should* be frightened of me!' said Rachel. 'When I become a Witch Dragwena said I'd enjoy killing you.' The moment she thought this Rachel sensed death-spells rise up in her mind. The spells told her she could already kill them all if she wanted. To Trimak she said, 'Get everyone ready to leave.'

'Listen Rachel,' Morpeth said, 'I know you are trans-forming into . . . *something*, but that does not necessarily mean you must become like Dragwena. Your instinct is still to protect us.'

Rachel hesitated. 'You mean I could fight her? Good Witch against bad Witch?'

'Yes. Why not? Perhaps you are not turning into Dragwena's kind of Witch at all. You might be able to protect the caves if need be. We must be careful to make the right decision. Think! Everything Dragwena showed you could be a lie. There may be no army approaching Latnap Deep.'

Grimwold knelt nearby. 'No. I sent someone to check. The Witch's army is coming, just as Rachel described it.'

Rachel gazed around the cave at the anxious faces of the Sarren.

'There isn't much time,' she said. 'I don't believe I can defeat the Witch. None of the spells I have learned show me how to do this. But I think I can get you all to safety, and then . . . I'll go somewhere alone, a long way off. It doesn't matter where. I'll wait until the transformation is complete, and see what happens to me. I daren't remain close to you all now. I can't take that risk. I'm thinking . . . if I can draw Dragwena off, fight her, weaken her somehow, maybe there will be a chance.'

Morpeth said firmly, 'We will never abandon you to Dragwena. We should stay together, no matter what happens.'

Trimak pulled out a knife. 'Morpeth is right. I once pledged to use this against you, Rachel.' He threw the knife down. 'That was a shameful thought. I sense Dragwena is deliberately trying to separate us. Stay. We will do what we can to protect you.'

Grimwold nodded, and all the Sarren fit enough to stand raised their swords and knelt before her.

'No,' Rachel said, her lip trembling. 'Look after Eric. Just don't let me or the Witch hurt him! Don't . . .' She trailed off, knowing Morpeth or the rest of the Sarren would never be able to protect Eric from Dragwena. The thought that she herself might hurt Eric was unbearable. Would Eric be safer with the Sarren? Or with her? Or – for a moment Rachel had a terrible vision of Eric all alone on Ithrea's snows, hiding from both her and Dragwena.

Eric tapped her on the shoulder. 'Hey, you.'

Rachel turned, and felt her four new jaws turn with her.

'I trust you,' he said. 'Don't go without me, Rachel. Don't leave me here.'

Rachel pulled him close. 'Aren't you scared of me?'

He grinned awkwardly. 'Well, a bit. Your teeth look flipping terrible.'

Rachel laughed – all four jaws joining in.

'But I've got this,' Eric said, stabbing his finger at the cave walls. 'I won't let Dragwena scare me. I *won't!*'

Rachel tried to smile. Was bringing Eric with her the right thing to do? Or was that what Dragwena wanted her to do?

Grimwold paced the floor of the cave. 'I don't see how you can get us safely from the caves, Rachel. Are you expecting the Sarren to run from this advancing army? Look at us!' He swept his arms around. 'Most can barely walk. Where will we go? Where will we hide?'

'Describe the weather,' Rachel said.

'What?'

'Is it dark outside?'

'Well, night, yes,' he replied impatiently. 'The sun set over an hour ago. So what? That will not protect us. Armath is full and shining like a demon down on us all. Dragwena's spies will spot us instantly.' He turned to Trimak. 'Let Rachel and Eric go if they must, but I say the Sarren should remain in Latnap Deep, and fight as best we can. Once we go to the surface, we'll be virtually defenceless. At least in the caves we can match steel with the Neutrana.'

Several Sarren muttered agreement.

'You won't need to run or fight,' Rachel said, scanning them. 'I have new powers now.'

Those Sarren who had serious wounds immediately stood up and shook themselves, their injuries gone. Rachel found the new spells she needed pouring effortlessly into her mind. Dragwena's spells, she realized. What was the best spell? What kind of spell could surprise Dragwena and enable them to escape undetected?

'Move everyone to the high corridors of Latnap Deep,' Rachel said, making up her mind.

'Where will you take us?' asked Trimak.

'Nowhere is safe. I'll take you as far from here as I can.'

As Rachel spoke a tooth sliced through her cheek – followed by a huge jaw. All the teeth stretched forward hungrily, trying to reach the Sarren. She felt something crawl over her gums and knew it was a spider, born in the saliva of her mouth. She did not try to spit it out, knowing other spiders were also being born who would replace it.

'Better hurry,' she said bitterly.

18

mawkmound

Rachel sat for a few minutes alone, making the spell she needed to leave the caves.

When it was ready the world above the Sarren altered. High in the night sky of Ithrea seven clouds moved furtively towards Latnap Deep. From the west they came, moving swiftly with the light breeze, though not so swiftly that their movement seemed different from any other cloud in the sky. For several miles they crept along the horizon, hugging the low hills, before rising in one great mass to obscure the moon.

'Now,' Rachel said to a sentry.

He lifted the doorway a few inches and glanced cautiously around. Dragwena's army approached, visible in all directions. The Sarren huddled in the corridors beneath the door, uncertain what to expect. A cold mist poured into the crack, covering everyone in a milky wetness.

'Don't be afraid,' Rachel's voice announced. 'Let the air surround you. I have summoned the mist to protect us. We will fly as a cloud. It will lift you into the sky. You will not fall, and the journey will be short.'

The next moment everyone's body reared up from the ground, as if a soft pillow had been placed beneath them. They all hung in the corridor, their feet a few inches above the floor.

'I'm ready,' said Rachel.

Led by her the Sarren floated slowly upwards into the night air – singly, as the doorway was too small for more than one to pass. Gently, like steam drifting from the mouth of a kettle, they poured out of Latnap Deep. By the time the last had been sucked out of the corridor Rachel herself was a thousand feet in the sky.

The long, thin column of greyness rotated in the air until it lay parallel to the horizon and flat. There it hovered. From a distance the column now looked exactly like a narrow grey cloud. No one could be seen or heard within. It drifted briefly in the light winds, travelling westwards with the other clouds in the sky, hiding the light of Armath and stars.

'Prepare yourselves!' Rachel exulted, her voice travelling throughout the length of the mist. 'We're departing!'

The cloud came to a stop, while those about it continued to roll west. A moment later, and silently, it shot south-westwards, keeping low to the ground. Inside the cloud many panicked as their bodies felt the lurch. The cloud gathered pace, cutting through the night. Rachel sent a warming spell through it, protecting everyone from the freezing wind.

A lone prapsy, flitting high in the sky, saw the cloud pass underneath. It blinked several times. 'What's that?' it asked itself, but the cloud had gone, and the prapsy instantly forgot what it had seen. Instead, it kept watch on the Witch's army marching below – Neutrana and the wolves would arrive at Latnap Deep within the hour.

The cloud, only briefly airborne, came to a halt over some gentle hills close to the South Pole of Ithrea: Mawkmound. Rachel's journey through Dragwena's mind had taught her everything about the planet. Here there were no spies, she knew. Nothing lived on Mawkmound except for a few scrawny trees, somehow defying the winds.

The cloud gently fell to the ground and dispersed, spilling Sarren into the snow. Several men leapt to their feet at once, their swords high and ready. Grimwold and Morpeth stayed close to Rachel, their eyes alert.

Morpeth walked the short distance between them and held her hands. 'Are you sure leaving is the right thing to do?' he asked. 'We would feel safer if you stayed.'

Rachel clacked her new teeth. 'What about these?'

'I could get used to them,' said Morpeth, lowering his gaze. 'I'm not sure I could get used to being without *you.*'

Rachel stroked his lean chin. 'You know, I think I preferred your ragged beard. I liked the old Morpeth better.'

'I'll grow it again for you,' he said earnestly. 'When you return.'

'I could change you back now if you like.'

Morpeth grinned. 'Oh, I don't know. I can see over

Trimak's head for the first time in over five hundred years. It's nice not having to look *up* at everyone all the time!'

'I never noticed that,' Rachel said, trying to hold back her tears. 'Whenever I watched, everyone was always looking up to *you*, Morpeth.'

As she hugged him, Morpeth said, 'Where's Eric going?'

Rachel saw Eric wandering away across a distant snow mound. 'Come back,' she shouted. 'Eric!'

Eric ignored her. 'Dragwena is here, or was here,' he said. 'Magic has a smell.' He lay face down in the snow and spread his arms. Sniffing, he drew circular patterns with his hands. 'I'll find her!'

'No, Eric!' Rachel cried.

Without warning, the snow in front of Eric parted and a figure uncoiled from the ground.

It was Dragwena.

Before Eric could defend himself the Witch struck him hard across the face, knocking him several feet across the snow. He lay there bleeding and unconscious. 'Time for you later, boy,' the Witch said.

Grimwold was the first to react. He and several Sarren threw themselves at the Witch. Dragwena fixed each with a swift look, throwing them hundreds of feet into the dark sky. Before they fell Rachel glanced up, held them in the air, pinned like wingless butterflies against the stars.

'Very good,' said Dragwena, 'but not quite good enough.' She sent a piercing thrust into Rachel's mind. The pain made Rachel lose control for a second. That moment was all it took for the Grimwold and the other Sarren to tumble from the skies.

Tumble to their deaths.

'There, child-hope,' said Dragwena. 'I shall enjoy many such deaths tonight. Did you think you could escape? You fool. You stink. Don't you realize that? You stink of magic. I could recognize your smell anywhere now. The cloud was a clumsy device, easily followed. As for Eric, I knew he would not be able to resist using his unusual gift to search for me. It is all so easy. You are only children. I will always be able to outwit you.'

Filled with horror, Rachel gazed at the dead Sarren. She prepared herself, expecting the Witch to attack her immediately. Instead, Dragwena said, 'You must know you can't defeat me. Why fight at all? Come to me willingly and I will spare the remainder of your friends. Even little Eric. I promise.'

Rachel instantly read the Witch's mind. Dragwena was momentarily unguarded. She blocked the spell, but not before Rachel had seen the truth: Dragwena planned to kill the Sarren savagely.

'You are *afraid*,' said Rachel. 'Nothing else would have made you promise something like that. You are lying. You are afraid of Eric, and you are afraid of me!'

Dragwena's confident mask fell away.

'Why are you so scared, Witch?'

Dragwena did not answer.

Rachel paused, for the first time really sensing their differences. 'I know why,' she realized. 'I'm not turning into your kind of Witch, am I?' She touched the four jaws on her face. 'In fact, I'm not . . . turning into a Witch *at all.*'

'You cannot resist much longer,' said Dragwena. 'Stop trying.'

Rachel cast her mind over everything that had happened

– the stabbing wound in the eye-chamber, Dragwena's insistence that it meant one thing only. As soon as Rachel questioned herself she understood the truth.

She faced Dragwena. 'It was *you* who tried to convince me I was becoming a Witch,' Rachel whispered. 'Over and over you kept saying I would be like you, think like you, look like you. And I believed it.' Rachel felt her hair, her arms, her four lips, and smiled. 'My own magic was developing. But magic doesn't know what it wants. Morpeth taught me that in the Breakfast Room, when I had to choose the colour of the bread. I forgot that simple lesson. Magic wants to be used. But it needs control. My magic ached to do *something*. Without realizing it I used it. I was so sure that I was becoming a Witch that the magic worked to do exactly that. If I had gone on believing, I might have become your kind of Witch in the end. That was your plan, all along.'

Instantly, Rachel returned her body to normal. She faced Dragwena with one set of teeth, her hair dark. 'You dumb, stupid Witch,' she said. 'I know what you want – to return to Earth to kill the Wizards and children. But you need my help, don't you? You can't do it alone. And I won't give it! A soothing voice won't work on me now, or your other tricks.' She looked without fear at Dragwena. 'I've learnt a lot. I can destroy myself if I need to. Whatever happens, you won't be able to turn me into your Witch. I'll *never* allow the dark verse to come true.'

Dragwena probed her mind. Rachel captured the thought and threw it back.

Dragwena shrieked her rage over and over, her voice echoing across Mawkmound.

'Then I hope you are ready for a battle, Rachel,' Dragwena hissed. 'You are useless to me now. I can't allow you to live.' Her tattooed eyes were fierce. 'A *real* fight! I have not had that pleasure for many years.'

'A fight to the death,' Rachel whispered.

'Of course.'

Rachel tried to remain calm, unprepared for this. 'I know some interesting spells now,' she said weakly.

'True,' said Dragwena. 'You borrowed them from *me*. But I know all the defences against those spells. I hope you have a new weapon, or our contest will be brief indeed.'

'That would be telling,' Rachel said.

'Now you *do* sound like a Witch,' Dragwena laughed. 'Brave little girl, do you know how many ways I have to kill you?'

Rachel nodded. 'I know everything, all your spells.'

'No,' Dragwena said softly. 'You know only what I *allowed* you to see. When Eric helped you find the death-spells I escaped before you found the deadliest. There are spells even more powerful than those: *Doomspells*. You have no defence against them, child. Doesn't that make you afraid?'

'Everything about you frightens me,' Rachel answered. 'But you would not be wasting time now unless you were also afraid of me.'

Dragwena appraised Rachel carefully, even admiringly. 'What a pity it is to have to destroy you,' she said. 'Still, if you exist there will be others to follow, no doubt. Larpskendya has bred magic in the children of Earth well. I thank him for that. I will not make the same mistakes with new children I made with you.' She stepped back. Her soul-snake licked diagonally across her face, a gesture to start the battle. 'Since you are game enough to challenge me, do you want to start the first spell, Rachel? I think you deserve that honour.'

Rachel glanced at Eric, still lying face down in the snow. She had to get Dragwena away from him as soon as possible – away from Mawkmound. She transformed into a raven and flapped into the sky.

Dragwena did not follow her immediately. Instead she turned to the Sarren. 'Watch the final scene,' she exulted. 'It will be the last thing you ever see. When I return I'm going to burn you all to death.'

A moment later a second raven cawed and sped after Rachel.

Everyone on Mawkmound gazed nervously after the black birds as they winged into the brooding night.

19

ðoomspell

Rachel was not ready to fight. She flew in a panic, wondering where to go. Where would be a safe place to hide? She shifted her mind to the Ragged Mountains, far from Mawkmound. She flew effortlessly amongst the peaks and valleys, wondering how to use the new spells, knowing Dragwena had practised them for thousands of years.

Safety first, Rachel thought. Become difficult to find. She stilled the sound of her beating wings to utter silence. Thick flocks of snow burned her eyes, so she flew blind, yet still saw the world with perfect clarity. Armath was bright, so she changed the colours of her upper body to reflect the moonlight. In the distance the Palace jutted from the ground, impenetrable black against the near black of the sky.

Would Dragwena find her quickly? Yes. Should she attack or defend? The spells gave her different answers when she asked them. Was there anything she could do that

Dragwena could not? Something new, a weapon Dragwena had never seen before? The spells offered no answer to this. Then Rachel realized she had not guarded her thoughts. Furious with herself, she blanked them out.

Instantly Dragwena appeared alongside her, wingtip to wingtip.

'Too late,' said Dragwena. 'You must think of the obvious things first, child. I could hear your thoughts yammering from Mawkmound. And now I know you have no secret weapon, either. You should never have revealed that. Keep me interested, or I'll tear your heart out.'

Rachel shifted rapidly and at random: from the Ragged Mountains to Dragwood; from Lake Ker to the Palace, hurrying, never staying in one place more than a few seconds. While she moved she also changed her shape, trying to throw off the Witch. Eventually, Rachel merged with the black rock of the Palace wall, becoming a grain of the wall itself, and waited there anxiously.

Part of the wall nearby spoke to her. 'Is this the best you can do? I know the pattern of your magic too well now for shape-shifting to throw me off. You caught me by surprise with your speck-of-dust trick in the eye-tower, but that can never work again. Hurry, I'm getting impatient. Dazzle me with your magic!'

Rachel leapt into a wolf prowling the Palace gardens. She took on its scent. She leapt into a frog, felt its slime and mingled that with the scent of wolf and other smells, always moving. For the first time she recognised the distinctive smell of her own magic, and removed it. Shifting many miles, she masked all the smells, becoming a wisp of odourless air, drifting aimlessly.

This time Dragwena did not find her for several minutes, and Rachel only knew when a ragged black claw ripped her from the sky.

'Interesting,' said Dragwena. 'What next?'

Rachel imitated the Witch, and held her inside a larger claw. Dragwena followed until the giant black hands blotted out Armath, claw after claw building in the sky.

At last Dragwena herself pulled them both to the ground. 'Is copying all you can think to do?' she asked, looking bored. 'I hoped for a more interesting battle than—'

Rachel leapt into the Witch's soul-snake. She gripped its mind, held its fangs and made it bite Dragwena's neck.

Dragwena screamed, then regained control, but Rachel already knew what she wanted to do next – the snake had been only a distraction. She made her body bright and created *thousands* of other Rachels, equally bright, in the air. For a moment the whole sky was so fierce with their incandescence that even on Mawkmound the Sarren saw it and wondered. Quickly, she made each pretend Rachel soar in several directions – into the earth, trees, rocks, water, and air. All the fake forms she kept in her mind, concentrating to make them as real as herself, giving them one scent, one weight, one pattern of breathing, one pulse, scattering them all to the corners of Ithrea.

From high in the sky above the Palace several Rachels glanced down. Amongst them, her true form saw the Witch, just for a moment, confused.

Then Dragwena appeared alongside her face, laughing loudly. Rachel screamed and it was this, only this, which gave her away. She noticed too late that Dragwena's laughing form had appeared alongside all the other Rachels.

'Oh, very good,' said Dragwena. 'Excellent! If only you had thought to make all the other Rachels scream it might have worked. But I suppose that's too much to ask. It takes many years of training to become a real Witch, and you do not have that long, do you?' She smiled. 'Keep trying. I don't wish to kill you just yet.'

Rachel shape-shifted all over Ithrea, trying to give herself time to consider something new. What else could she try? Come on, she told herself. Think! Something *completely* different . . .

Dragwena casually followed Rachel's shape-shifting. She took her time, enjoying the game, hoping there would be a few more interesting surprises. Rachel had stopped, Dragwena realized, in of all places Dragwood. The Witch glided towards the earth, knowing exactly where Rachel had landed. But instead of the dark trees the Witch found a tropical forest waiting for her. Instead of dark earth between the trees she found sweet grasses bursting with life. And sitting cross-legged amongst the grass fronds was a Wizard with many-coloured eyes.

'Larpskendya!' gasped Dragwena.

'I told you I would always protect this world,' said Larpskendya. 'Did you think I would allow you to hunt Rachel down?'

Dragwena collapsed to her knees, burying her head in her hands. 'This can't be true!'

The instant the Witch averted her eyes, Larpskendya's body disappeared. Where it had been, a needle-sharp blade hovered in the air. Rachel controlled the blade, a combination of all the fast death spells she could muster. She launched it while Dragwena was confused, unprepared, and sliced into the Witch's body, tearing it to shreds.

The wind blew the tatters of Dragwena's remains across the snow, scattering them. Rachel transformed back into a girl. For some time she examined the shreds of bone and flesh and clothing, poking the remains gingerly with her feet, hardly daring to believe it had worked.

Then, behind her, Rachel heard a slow handclap.

Dragwena stood there, unharmed. 'Oh, well done,' she said. 'Brilliant! What a fantastic Witch you would have made. What daring! To seek out what I feared most and use it. I only just managed to shape-shift into a tree at the last moment.' She bowed elaborately. 'It is an honour to fight you. Shall we continue?'

Rachel watched the Witch's expression. There was no fear there, only pleasure and enjoyment of the battle. Rachel knew that Dragwena had not even started to fight seriously. At any moment Dragwena could launch an attack. Rachel ignored the spells clamouring in her mind and tried recalling Dragwena's memories. There had to be something else she could use! What was Dragwena's weakness? Where could the Witch never follow her? Of course!

Rachel transformed into a rocket, aiming for the edge of the sky. The clouds scudded over her face, the air growing thinner.

'What are you trying now?' asked Dragwena, taking the same form, following her upward.

Rachel focused on shutting out her thoughts, but Dragwena sensed she was doing exactly that and read her intention.

The Witch slammed them both into the ground below.

'Idiot,' Dragwena said. 'If you had not shut your mind, I would not have bothered to read it until too late. You might have escaped! A wasted chance. Since you knew I cannot leave Ithrea, why didn't you just imagine yourself already outside the planet? I could never have followed you. But you did the obvious thing: you made yourself just *fly fast*. You are still thinking like a child, Rachel.'

Rachel immediately tried to picture herself in space, outside the world. Her body hurtled upwards, then crumpled like paper – an invisible shield created by Dragwena held her in. Rachel recovered, flew across the sky, desperately hoping for a crack in the shield. There was none. The stars beckoned above, achingly close. Rachel clawed at their winking light, seeking a way through.

The Witch appeared alongside. 'I think our little battle is almost over,' she said. 'I was wrong about being able to use you, but perhaps I should have concentrated on your brother from the beginning.' She smiled, pulling Rachel's face close. '*Eric* has much I can use. With training, I sense he might be able to remove the bonds of magic Larpskendya has wrapped around this world. It may be *Eric*, after all, who helps me fulfil the dark ver—'

Rachel breathed a blinding spell at Dragwena. Their heads were so close that Dragwena did not have time to shut her eyes. For a moment blades of emerald attacked her face; then they vanished, leaving the Witch unharmed.

'I know defences against all your spells,' the Witch whispered. 'Eric will not fight like you. He is so young. He will be much easier to persuade.'

Rachel screamed and shifted again, but this time

Dragwena did not follow. She simply ripped Rachel from the sky and dragged them both back to Mawk-mound.

Rachel saw Morpeth and Trimak and the rest of the Sarren turn towards them expectantly. Eric lay in Morpeth's arms, still unconscious.

'See their anxious little faces?' said Dragwena. 'I want them all to see you crushed, to see the end of their child-hope. Then I will kill Morpeth and Trimak slowly, over a hundred years perhaps. Eric can help me. The others are not important.' She laughed. 'Where is your precious Larps-kendya now? Where is the Wizard who promised to protect you?'

Rachel had one last desperate idea. She craned her neck, pointing towards Armath. She drew a deep breath – and shouted out the verse of hope.

For a moment the air rippled delicately. Everyone on Mawkmound felt it, even the Witch. Rachel and the Sarren waited hopefully, but something was missing. The words faded in the night breeze, and Armath shone coldly above.

Rachel bowed her head, completely defeated. Defiance, bravery, all of her magic – none of it seemed any use now. Where was Larpskendya? *Where was he?* Rachel glanced at the Sarren huddled across Mawkmound and the small face of Eric cradled in Morpeth's arms, and could think of nothing left to try.

'Prepare to die, girl,' said Dragwena. 'I am summoning the Doomspell.'

The Witch walked slowly to the centre of Mawkmound and raised her arms. She incanted spells in the language of

Ool, her home world. Rachel knew a few of the words from the death spells in her mind, but most she did not recognize. Here, she realised, was one of the deadliest spells Dragwena had never revealed – a killing spell of incalculable power. Rachel searched for something – anything – to defend herself.

The Doomspell arrived slowly. Dragwena knew there was no need for haste now. From the frozen wastes of the north a gigantic storm-whirl tore itself from a corner of the world. Rachel saw it from many miles away, an inferno of blasting rage. As she watched, the storm-whirl spread out to cover the entire sky. Its immense shadow bulged over the land, obliterating snow and stars. Over the Ragged Mountains the storm-shadow poured and Armath, shining there, was consumed by it. Mountains and streams were devoured and a wind rose that began to blow fiercely over Mawkmound.

The Sarren were terrified, but they did not scatter. Instead Trimak and a procession of Sarren solemnly crossed the snows of Mawkmound towards Rachel, their bodies bent against the wind. Morpeth hesitated for a moment, glancing first at Eric, then Rachel. Eventually, he carried Eric some distance away across the snows. Rachel saw him place his jacket under Eric's head, lower him gently in the snow and mutter three words. Not a protection spell, Rachel realized – Morpeth knew his magic was too weak to protect Eric. It was simply an apology, one Eric would probably never hear. Morpeth kissed Eric on the forehead and quickly caught up with the others.

All the Sarren now surrounded Rachel. Those with swords pointed them at Dragwena.

The Witch laughed. 'Swords? How touching.'

The vast storm-whirl finally reached Mawkmound. It hovered over Dragwena's head, a mass of coiling black cloud as wide as the horizon. Dragwena traced a shape in the air. Instantly, the cloud changed shape, condensing into a single thin grinding tunnel of wind, the thickness of rope. Dragwena dislocated her jaw. It flopped onto her chin, and the tunnel leapt inside her mouth. She shuddered with ecstasy as it poured inside her throat.

The Witch closed her mouth and smiled at Rachel. 'Ready?'

'Yes!' the Sarren closest to Dragwena bellowed.

Dragwena pointed her mouth at him and released the Doomspell.

A thick pillar of black smoke streamed at extraordinary speed from her lips. Inside the smoke a thousand teeth rushed to the surface.

Rachel placed several rings of protection around the Sarren, but it made no difference. The first Sarren hit by the smoke was torn apart. Knowing all the others would be killed, Rachel transported the remaining Sarren to safety at the edge of Mawkmound – and met the full force of the smoke and teeth alone.

She shielded her body with several spells, but the teeth inside gnawed relentlessly. Rachel fought them with every-thing she knew: with defensive spells, with killing spells, with incantations of paralysis and, finally, as the teeth burst through, even with her nails.

But it was no use. Dragwena cackled with joy as the teeth began to eat Rachel's lips and eyes.

20

MANAG

Rachel felt the teeth tearing lumps from her face. They shredded her arms and legs. They attacked her neck and heart, seeing the quickest way to kill her, chewing hungrily at her flesh, whispering the words of the Doomspell, willing her to die.

Rachel endured everything. Her whole mind was focused on a single spell to deaden her body to the pain. She waited and waited until all the teeth clung to her body. At last, when she could hear the whisper of the last jaw of the Doomspell, its meaning was fully revealed.

Rachel made fists of both her hands and unhinged her jaw. Her chin dropped and her mouth gaped wide. Through a gargle of blood and air she choked out the words she needed. Immediately, the teeth stopped biting. The black column of smoke and teeth rushed inside her throat, filling her.

Rachel's torn and bloodied body gazed evenly at Dragwena. 'Get ready,' she muttered. 'Larpskendya taught me in the dream-sleep that there is a spell of goodness for every spell of evil, Witch. You'd better start running before it catches you!'

She coughed. Blue smoke emerged from her mouth, moving slowly towards Dragwena.

'What is this?' asked Dragwena, backing away nervously. 'You cannot use the Doomspell. It is mine alone.'

Rachel pressed her chest with both hands, continuing to cough, and the blue smoke advanced more thickly. She incanted words backwards in the Witch's tongue. The spell flooded from her lips and followed the smoke.

A look of understanding suddenly gleamed in Dragwena's eye. 'A reversal,' she whispered. 'You are reversing the Doomspell. Bad to good: no, it cannot work.'

Dragwena continued to retreat. The first wisp of smoke touched her leg. She screamed in pain – and ran.

The words streamed from Rachel. Dragwena raised her arms and flew upward. A tendril of smoke yanked her back and fisted her into the ground. The rest of the blue column rapidly encircled Dragwena, pouring into her nose and throat and eyes. There were no teeth inside, but the Witch wailed and writhed under the onslaught as if inhaling fire.

Then, as suddenly as they had started, the words ceased. The reversal spell was at an end. As it finished Rachel's wounds vanished. She closed her mouth and the last blue vapours disappeared.

Everyone looked at Dragwena.

She lay in torment on the ground, her whole body burning in a blue flame which still reached deep inside.

But the Witch was not dead. With a huge effort she lifted her head into the air, and rasped: 'Manag . . . Manag . . .' The smoke poured back out of Dragwena's throat like glue, flicked out by her tongue.

It rose into the air and formed into a clawed creature with green eyes and a mouth that spread across all Mawkmound.

The Sarren looked desperately to Rachel for an explanation, but she had no understanding or answer.

Dragwena sat up. A bright green light ran over her body, snuffing out the last of the blue flames. 'Did you think the Doomspell is only a few flashing teeth?' she scoffed. 'It is countless spells, whatever I need it to be. This time a reversal will not work.'

Dragwena kissed the air. Rachel's body stiffened, outlined by a ring of flickering green fire. Understanding, the Manag opened its great claws and dived to rip her apart . . .

Morpeth ran towards Eric, shaking him over and over.

'Get up! Wake up!' he pleaded.

At last Eric raised his head and got clumsily to his feet. He stumbled towards Rachel and stood in front of her, tiny against the Manag's hugeness. Pointing with both hands, he punched holes in the creature's frame, somehow holding it back. But the spell that formed the Manag kept changing, inching closer, defying him. At last its breath swotted Eric to the ground. He fell on top of Rachel, still wildly jabbing his fingers.

'I can't stop it!' he cried. 'I can't stop it! It's made up of millions of spells. There are too many. I can't stop them all!'

'Sing the verse of hope,' Rachel told him. 'Sing it! Sing it!'

Eric pressed both his hands into the face of the Manag. He twisted his head towards the Endellion Ocean and sang in a high voice:

> *'Dark girl she will be,*
> *Enemies to set free,*
> *Sing in harmony,*
> *From sleep and dawn-bright sea,*
> *I will arise,*
> *And behold you childish glee.'*

The Manag warily opened its eyes.

'Sing it again!' Rachel shouted.

'Dark girl . . .' Eric began, and this time Rachel joined him, two voices singing in harmony. Over and over they sang, not stopping, louder and louder, until they heard an ancient sound rumble from its sleep – an immense heart thudding across the night.

The Manag stopped. It hovered over Rachel, rearing back, and turned uncertainly towards Dragwena.

'Finish it!' the Witch shrieked. 'Kill her! Kill her!'

The Manag flexed its claws, still hesitating.

'Destroy her!' Dragwena commanded. 'I created you. I demand it! Do it!'

Lunging forward, the Manag opened its great jaws within inches of Rachel's head, but still withheld its attack.

The Witch raged wildly at the creature, and it groaned with the agony of her words, yet something else tugged at the Manag's will. It continued to hover, glancing first at Dragwena, then at Rachel. Finally it ignored them both and turned its apprehensive eyes westward. And now every-one's eyes followed it, for a remarkable transformation was taking place.

In the middle of the night, with Armath at its zenith high in the sky, a sunrise was beginning in the far reaches of the world.

At first there was only a dim orange glow over the western mountains. But soon the sun rose in all its glory and ascended at an impossible speed into the sky. It was not the meagre creamy sun that had shone for so long on Ithrea. This sun was wild and golden. Almost painfully bright, it heaved itself into the air, pouring through the clouds of Ithrea for the first time in thousands of years. The Sarren gaped in wonder as they followed it, incandescent beams flashing off their cheekbones. Dragwena staggered and uttered an agonised cry, unable to bear the touch of the sun's rays. She called the Manag and cowered beneath it, hiding her head between her knees.

The Sarren continued to watch events unfold. High in the sky, beyond the rising sun, the night air was still dark – then something equally impossible happened: Armath, the great moon, fell from its place low over the Ragged Mountains, splashing with a mighty explosion into the Endellion Ocean.

'What's happening?' cried Trimak.

'I don't know,' Morpeth said, watching the tremendous plume of sizzling water thrown up by the moon.

The green ring of fire surrounding Rachel vanished. As she rushed across to the others Morpeth saw points of light plummeting in her eyes.

'Look!' Trimak cried. 'Look at the stars!'

In the sky above Ithrea, one by one, and then in their hundreds, like points of light on wallpaper, the stars were falling from their appointed places, following Armath into the ocean. Meanwhile, the sun continued its galloping ascent until it stood high above their heads. Bright daylight now swept across Mawkmound.

Dragwena pulled her dress over her face, her eyes bleeding.

Morpeth was too astonished to care what had happened to the Witch. He pointed towards the waters into which the last of the stars had sunk. 'How can we see the ocean?' he whispered. 'It should be frozen.'

Their answer was not long in coming. The Endellion Ocean was *rising*, barely noticeable until now as it had such a long way to climb before toppling over the western mountains. As they watched its writhing waters spilled over the highest summits, flowing towards them at devastating speed, swallowing the land.

Morpeth pointed eastward. There, in a far corner of the world, where no Sarren had ever travelled, an even mightier ocean also swept towards Mawkmound.

'Why aren't I scared?' asked Trimak. 'This should be terrifying.'

All the Sarren realized they were filled with awe, not terror. But a despairing Dragwena called weakly to the Manag. She could barely raise her head. The Manag shrank and moved to surround the Witch, trying to use its bulk to shield her from the rays of the sun.

Rachel whispered to Eric.

He giggled and they both turned to face the advancing waters.

'*Come Larpskendya!*' they sang together. '*Come from sleep and dawn-bright sea!*'

And Larpskendya came at last: from the tumultuous foaming ocean a silver bird rose from the depths. He was of such size that the waters could hardly contain his beating wings. With slow, massive motion he swept from the waves and headed towards Mawkmound. He boomed out the words of the verse of hope, filling the air with a sound whose loveliness cannot be named. And his many-coloured eyes blazed with beauty.

Dragwena met his stare. As soon as she did so Larpskendya locked her in a gaze of fear – in his eyes she saw a million grim-faced children, sharpening their knives against a stone wall. She shrieked and pointed.

'Kill it!' she instructed the Manag. 'Kill the Wizard!'

Without hesitation, the great shadow left her shoulder. Larpskendya turned to meet the creature. As he drew closer the Manag dwindled until it was just a point of swift darkness against his dripping breast. A mile above the ocean they met and Larpskendya, hardly even needing to open his bill, ripped the Manag from the sky.

Dragwena lurched with pain as her spell-creature was devoured.

'I'll kill you yet!' she roared, racing towards the Sarren, her face contorted by fear and rage. 'Even in defeat I'll destroy you!'

'Form a guard!' cried Trimak, and the Sarren rushed to put themselves between the children and the Witch.

Dragwena lunged past the Sarren, unscathed by their swords. She ripped Eric from Rachel's hands and ran to a low mound. Rachel fired wounding spells, but Dragwena fought through them, heaving herself and Eric across the snow.

Larpskendya swooped across the ocean. He flew with immense speed straight towards the Witch, but Dragwena already held Eric close – she knew there was time to snap his neck.

'See this!' Dragwena howled at the silver bird. 'You cannot save him! One more child I *will* kill!'

As she tightened her grip Eric uttered one word.

Dragwena twitched with pain. She dropped Eric, staggering backwards. Blood poured from her ear. 'What is this?' she rasped. 'An *unmaking* spell? No. I . . . will not be denied . . . by a child!' Dragwena fumbled to retrieve him, but Eric danced easily aside and went to the safety of Rachel's embrace.

The Witch could not follow. She lay writhing on the ground and then, clenching her fists and fighting to regain control, she shrieked as she started to transform: her blood-red skin peeled and she was a snake; and then it peeled again and she was a mollusc, and a raven, and a wolf, and a black monster writhing with serpents; and a hideous creature between whose splintered teeth spiders rushed to escape. The Witch merged into all the forms she had ever taken, faster and faster, until the transformations were so rapid that they blurred together and her screaming voice became unrecognizable.

But Dragwena was not finished. Somehow, through an overwhelming hatred, she managed to leap from the confusion, black claws outstretched.

Rachel howled, and with the sound of it Larpskendya swept from the sky. His head raked the ground, plucking the Witch from the earth.

Everyone watched as Dragwena, a speck inside the enormous beak, somehow held it open. She gasped, trembling with the effort, her teeth slashing, trying to string together all her knowledge into a single venomous spike of death. But Larpskendya had no fear of Dragwena's magic. Gradually his beak closed until the Witch's arms buckled and her knees were squeezed against her bursting chest. At last, Dragwena could no longer endure and her spine snapped. She unhinged her jaw and uttered a final despairing cry.

'Sisters!' she shrieked. *'Revenge me!'*

Even as Larpskendya's beak shut, killing the Witch, a tiny green light rose into the air where Dragwena's body had been. Unnoticed by anyone, the light flew directly into the sky. It pierced the outer atmosphere and shot into space. Once there it snaked towards a distant star, towards a watchful, Witch-filled world . . .

21

the choice

Everyone on Mawkmound gazed in awe as Larpskendya hovered above them, his great wings thrashing the air. Eric ran across the mound and jumped up to nuzzle the huge bird's wing. But it was to Rachel alone that Larpskendya turned his many-coloured eyes.

And, in that brief moment, the Wizard imparted many things: an apology for the suffering he had allowed; a choice they all must make; and happiness, enormous tear-joyful happiness for what was to come. Finally, Larpskendya bent close to Rachel, touching her face. An extraordinary feeling shuddered through her.

'A gift,' he said. 'A gift no human has ever been trusted with.'

Rachel trembled, understanding it, and trying to find the words to thank him. But immediately Larpskendya wrapped around the gift a task and a warning.

At last the Wizard turned his head and soared upward and away into the western sky.

'Goodbye, Larpskendya,' Rachel said, casting her eyes down because she could not bear to look so closely at his magnificence.

Silence descended on Mawkmound as everyone else watched him disappear slowly into the distance, his tail dappled by golden sunbeams.

And then two immense shadows blocked out all the sunlight.

'Watch out!' cried Trimak.

Even as the children and Sarren gazed after Larpskendya, the oceans of Ithrea had continued to sweep towards them. Suddenly, like a flood to end the world, the mighty waves came crashing down on Mawkmound. There was no time for anyone to protect themselves, nowhere to run or hide. But instead of crushing everyone the oceans halted at the edge of the mound, and cast something towards them more gently than falling snow.

Morpeth gasped as, of all things, a Neutrana guard slid from the waters and landed by his feet. The man got up, grinning widely. 'I'm . . . free!' he cried, rubbing his head. Bowing in several directions, he announced his name to one and all.

'Free?' laughed a Sarren. 'You're a bit late for the fight, that's certain!' He pulled the newcomer away from the water. 'Where did you come from, anyway?'

But before he could answer, another passenger of the waves was unceremoniously dumped onto the mound.

'Muranta!' gasped Trimak, helping his wife up. 'How did you come to be here?'

'How do I know?' she replied irritably. 'One moment I'm at home, worrying about *you*; the next I'm picked up by that – that great wave' – she jerked her arm back – 'and now I'm . . . wherever this freezing place is!' She brushed water from her dress.

But there was hardly time to dwell on this either, as an awkward Leifrim toppled from the waves. A surge deposited him by Fenagel's feet, and his daughter bent to kiss him.

'This isn't possible!' said Morpeth. 'They couldn't. It's—'

'It's true!' Rachel shouted, her eyes filled with tears of joy. 'Watch!'

And now everything happened at once. All manner of creatures, animal and human, tumbled from the waves so quickly that no one pair of eyes could take it all in. Sarren came, adults and children from all over Ithrea; and bumping alongside were Neutrana, crowds of them, their expressions filled with surprise. On wave after wave they arrived, from everywhere Sarren or Neutrana lived, the waters delivering them up to Mawkmound.

Wolves came in their multitudes, Scorpa at their head, their great grey flanks covered in brine. Prapsies spilt on the surf, flitting about and speaking their usual nonsense.

They came and came, and still it never ended. Hundreds of thousands surged from the waves, until Mawkmound became a seething mass of all creatures who had once bent their backs to the will of Dragwena. Ronnocoden arrived with his proud eagle companions, beating their sodden wings and singing their hearts out, after a silence of centuries. And extraordinary creatures came that nobody knew – creatures that had lived and bred under the snows of Ithrea, forgotten in the darkness for untold years. They wriggled and slid and crawled over each other, teeth flashing, covering their sensitive eyes from a sun they had never seen.

Eventually it was at an end, and the waters retreated a little way, giving everyone a chance to spread out.

And how they spread out!

The wolves bayed and leapt onto the new wet grass that sprang from nowhere at their feet. Children petted the wolves, and raced after them in circles trying to stroke their fur, but hardly able to catch up. So instead the eagles let them climb on their backs and made short flights over the land, teasing the prapsies as they passed.

And the Sarren and Neutrana, for some reason over which they had no control, began to dance and sing and whirl together. Their voices clamoured with the birds in the air, who did not stop singing for a second, until the noise of shouting and laughter and baying and twittering became so great that the earth shook with it and boomed its happiness back.

Morpeth moved alongside Rachel and Eric and wistfully said the words:

> 'Dark girl she will be,
> Enemies to set free,
> Sing in harmony,
> From sleep and dawn-bright sea,
> I will arise,

Rachel looked lovingly into his eyes:

> 'And behold your childish glee.'

And she was right, for even as the Sarren and eagles and wolves and other creatures leapt and skittered and danced they slowly transformed, until they became children and puppies and eagle-young. Prapsies shook off their baby-faces and returned to being crow-chicks, their red mouths crying out for their mothers. Morpeth changed into a sandy-haired boy with bright blue eyes, and Trimak grinned from his dimpled chubby cheeks.

'Well,' said Eric, shaking his head and looking at no one in particular. 'Flipping heck!'

'Exactly!' laughed Trimak.

'But what happens now?' asked Morpeth. 'We're all children again. What are we going to do?'

With these words, as if he had initiated a spell, which indeed he had, though he did not know it, all the creatures of Ithrea fell silent and turned towards Rachel.

She traced a shape in the air. A doorway appeared, which led to the back of a cellar with thick stone walls.

'What home will it be?' she said. 'Ithrea or Earth? Larpskendya has given each of you a choice.'

A choice? The creatures of Ithrea stared blankly at each other. They had known the servitude of the Witch for so long that they hardly knew how to react. And how to choose? For nearly all of the children Earth was just a dim memory. The animals had never known Earth at all. To them Ithrea *was* home.

Puppies sat on their tails and yelped in confusion. Chicks huddled, cheeping uncertainly; and the strangest creatures of Ithrea slurped in their own tongues, wondering what to do. At last all the animals turned for advice to the children, but the former Sarren and Neutrana were bewildered. As Rachel and Eric watched, thousands of boys and girls started urgently questioning each other, trying to recall their lives on Earth, the families and friends who once shared their days.

And slowly, painfully, *all* began to remember.

'Oh Rachel,' said Eric. 'Look. They're . . . crying.'

It began as a few stifled sobs, but soon whole groups were weeping uncontrollably. They limped across Mawkmound, or fell to their knees, each child in its own world of grief as the images and words and feelings came hauntingly back: of long-dead parents, brothers and sisters, and priceless friends they would never see or touch again.

A young Leifrim, with spiky jet black hair, screwed up his face.

'My mother,' he said. 'I remember the way she held me, but—' He gazed about shamefully, hoping someone might help. 'What was her name? I can't—'

Fenagel put her arms around her father. She had been born on Ithrea. All her life she had known only its dark snows. But many had no children to comfort them, for the Witch had only allowed a few close servants this honour. Within minutes all the children on Mawkmound were bent in private tears, or clutching what loved ones they could find, gripped by an overwhelming sense of loss.

'No,' pleaded Eric. 'Rachel, please stop them. Use a spell. It wasn't meant to end like this. Surely Larpskendya didn't mean it to end like this.'

'Wait,' she said, her own eyes filled with tears. 'Larpskendya told me this would happen. It's not just dead families they're grieving for, Eric. It's what the Witch did to them, all those centuries of suffering.' She smiled through her tears. 'What happens next will be amazing.'

The anguish of the children went on for a long time. It

went on for longer than it had taken Ithrea's oceans to deliver them all to Mawkmound. It went on for as long as the last child still had the strength left to cry. Finally, the weeping ended and Mawkmound fell silent. The silence was so deep that even the Prapsy chicks seemed to realize they should not babble. They furled their stubby wings over their beaks and waited.

And a gentle wind stirred on Mawkmound.

Trimak was the first to notice it touch his cheek. It dried his tears, spreading warmth.

'Look!' he cried, pointing everywhere.

Until this moment no one had bothered to wonder what might be happening beyond Mawkmound. Now they saw the ocean waters had retreated into the far distance, melting all the snow. Black soil, scarred and lifeless, covered the whole world. Ithrea was naked. Even the grass had been torn from the ground. Not a single thing grew or stirred. A child sighed and her voice echoed across the barren emptiness.

'No,' whispered Trimak. 'Is this what we waited for all those centuries? Even the snows were more comfort than this.'

Rachel laughed. 'Then wish for something else!'

'Flowers?' he muttered. 'That would be something at least.'

Instantly, plant buds started shooting between his feet. He jumped aside and they quickly filled his footprints.

'What colour flowers?' asked Rachel. 'And what shape? What smell should they have? And how many?'

'How should I know?' said Trimak, trying not to tread on them. 'What do I know about flowers?'

Rachel grinned. 'Are you giving up already?'

'Nice ones,' he said, feebly. 'Pretty ones. What were their names? Oh . . . I don't know!'

The buds continued to spread out, but they stayed tight shut – waiting.

'White roses!' said Fenagel. 'Purple daffodils. Green daisies. Red – oh!'

The buds were opening into all the flowers named. They continued to spread across Mawkmound and beyond.

'Stop!' yelled Morpeth, and the flowers stopped.

'Roses that sing!' cried Trimak, and immediately the white roses began a tuneless whine, their petals flapping back and forth. 'Don't sing like me!' he told them. 'Sing beautifully, you stupid things!' And so the roses changed their tune. The sound was not beautiful, but it did sound stupid.

'Magic doesn't know what beautiful means,' said Rachel. 'Tell it, *you* stupid thing!'

Trimak fell about laughing, but others took up the challenge.

'Like happiness!'

'Like cockatoos!'

'Like gurgling babies!'

The flowers started singing like all these things.

'How can this be happening?' said Morpeth. Nearby, a girl pressed her ear against a humming buttercup.

Rachel winked. 'Magic. Larpskendya's given you everything you need.'

'To do what?' he said.

'To do what you like!' said Rachel. 'Don't be shy, Morpeth. Imagine something!'

Morpeth was lost for words. He nervously created a tiny sun in his palm and blew it into the sky.

'Oh, think *bigger* than that,' said Rachel. 'Look at what the others are doing already!'

Morpeth lifted his eyes and, wherever he gazed, he saw children everywhere testing their imaginations, making up the rest of Ithrea. Forests with legs marched up the slopes of the Ragged Mountains. Fenagel ran across the mound, jewels following behind her like obedient pets. Children wrote their names in the sky. Melon-shaped mountains began glistening in the distance, spitting out pips like volcanoes. A large stone rolled across to one boy and offered him a selection of sweets. As for the flowers, the first creations of the new Ithrea, they were soon forgotten, but they didn't care. They just carried on singing loudly. That is, until Muranta told them to hush. After this they just whispered.

In the distance, Eric saw a fire-breathing dragon rise up from Lake Ker. Amongst the other bizarre forms appearing everywhere he would hardly have noticed, but this dragon was heading for the little eaglets.

'Hey, cut it out,' he warned the giggling prapsy chicks, but the eagles had already turned the dragon into a beak. This chased the startled prapsies until they sent it pecking back after the eagles.

Eric said to Rachel, 'Isn't this all getting a bit . . . dangerous?'

'They can't hurt each other,' she told him. 'Larpskendya wouldn't allow it. Let them play. It's so long since they did.' Some toasted marmalade hovered in front of her mouth. 'You do like marmalade, I hope,' the toast said.

Rachel turned to see Morpeth smiling at her.

The craze of pure imagination went on and on, until some part of Ithrea belonged to everyone. Eventually Trimak called a brief halt to the magic and mischief.

'I know what I want!' he thundered. 'To stay! Ithrea is my home now. I have made my choice.'

'Brilliant choice!' boomed a voice. It came from Hoy Point in the Ragged Mountains. The ancient mountain lifted a cap and waved it enthusiastically. Behind Trimak a boy chuckled. 'Sorry,' he said, slightly embarrassed. 'Couldn't resist it.'

After this, with Ithrea beckoning with all its absurd wild loveliness, it was not long before most of Ithrea's creatures had also made their choice. Some asked for more information about Earth, but when they found out there was no magic on that world they soon lost interest.

To Rachel and Eric's surprise a handful of creatures did decide to return with them. A few deep-dwelling worms wrapped themselves around Eric's legs, and wouldn't let go. Scorpa peeled herself from a group of puppies and licked Rachel's knees so violently that she kept falling over. A pair of prapsies, for no particular reason, or at least no reason anyone could understand, crept onto her feet and mumbled something about flitting amongst new skies.

'I thought they'd just be normal crow chicks now,' said Eric. 'How come they can talk?'

'Larpskendya wouldn't take that gift from them,' Rachel said. 'The puppies can talk too. They just prefer barking.'

'That's right,' Scorpa said to Eric. 'Don't try petting me. I hate all that stuff.'

'I wouldn't think of it,' replied Eric, who had just been about to do so.

Ronnocoden suddenly flapped onto Rachel's shoulder. He stared imperiously over the heads of the prapsy chicks, as if they were beneath his attention.

Late in the first morning of the new Ithrea a simple ceremony took place. The bodies of Grimwold and the other warriors killed by Dragwena had been taken by the retreating waves, but they were not forgotten. Trimak marked the spot they had fallen with a cluster of swords: one for each of the warriors. He thrust the blades into the rich soil, and angled the hilts inwards, towards each other.

As the afternoon drew on, Eric said, 'I don't think any of the Sarren are coming back home with us, Rachel. I don't blame them.'

But he was wrong. One child decided to return to Earth.

Rachel watched for hours as he hugged and cried, and laughed and wept again, saying his farewells – farewells to countless other Sarren and Neutrana he had known. So many people, Rachel thought. Five hundred years worth of people. How do you say goodbye, a *final* goodbye, to those you have loved and shared all life and death with for that long?

At last, when he had embraced Trimak for what seemed like an hour, a leaving almost without words, as if they were not necessary, Morpeth was ready.

His face was so messed with tears that Rachel could barely meet his gaze.

'Are you sure you want to go?' she asked. 'All your friends are here.'

'Not all my friends,' said Morpeth, earnestly. He touched the lids of her many-coloured eyes and gave her a sly glance. 'You didn't just imagine these. I saw what happened when Larpskendya touched you,' he said. 'You have the Wizard's look now. Did you think I wouldn't notice? Larpskendya's given you a present, hasn't he?'

'Shush,' she said. 'I can't say what it is. A gift – and a task to perform.'

Morpeth clapped his hands in delight, then turned to see what wonders he had missed being created on Ithrea during the last few seconds.

'This is unbelievable!' he roared.

'And ridiculous!' laughed Eric. 'What's *that* supposed to be?' He pointed at a fat pig floating in the sky. It lay comfortably on a cloud, wearing sunshades, sipping lemonade. Below, on the ground, a little girl frowned up in concentration, obviously wondering what to make up next. 'That's just totally stupid,' said Eric.

'Oh, I quite like it,' smiled Morpeth. 'But look over there. Now that *really* does look stupid.'

And they stood pointing and peering at everything: burbling streams filled with frogs and skipping dragons and galloping rainbow-coloured horses, and things none of them could recognize, all growing and fading in the yellow-gleamy sky. Fish armed with rods hauled imitation Witches out of Lake Ker, and the comfortable fat pig now had a friend – the little girl, clutching its curly tail, was flying around Mawkmound. Instantly several other children joined in, or flew off in other directions, racing into the distance. Within seconds they were in every corner of the world, changing it, pouring out their imaginations, conquering the ancient winter world of the Witch.

Eventually, the sun began to set and one boy created a new moon. As he lifted his arms it rose slowly over the land, a crafty smile on its face. He pointed at the sky and a new constellation of stars gleamed warmly down.

Morpeth tried to take the whole fantastic world in with one last wide-ranging look, but it was not possible. Too much was happening.

'It's got, well, everything,' said Eric.

'No, it hasn't,' Rachel corrected him. 'Something's missing. Something dark and cold.'

Morpeth blasted, 'That's right! No *snow!*'

They all laughed, realizing that Ithrea's dark snows were gone forever.

'We don't really have to go straightaway, do we?' Morpeth almost begged. 'There's so much to see, so much to do!'

'I'm sorry,' said Rachel. 'Larpskendya told me it would be dangerous to leave the gateway open for too long. We must leave now.'

'Why?'

'I can't say.'

'Is it anything to do with Witches?'

Rachel nodded tightly. 'Don't ask anything else. I can't tell you until we get back.'

'If I go,' said Morpeth, 'can I ever come back?'

'I'm not sure,' said Rachel solemnly. 'Larpskendya didn't tell me. We might never be able to return to Ithrea.'

Morpeth nodded glumly and looked back at Trimak. Most of the other children had started heading off in different directions, but Trimak had not moved. He stood dead still at the centre of Mawkmound, his arm around his wife, Muranta. Rachel knew he would not take his eyes off Morpeth until his old friend left.

Morpeth walked reluctantly towards the cellar doorway, still glancing over his shoulder to see what the next child might conjure up. A worm took the opportunity to slip from Eric's leg and wrap itself around Morpeth's shin.

'Quick, then,' Morpeth said, clenching Rachel's hand. 'Before the worm and I change our minds.'

Rachel took one step inside the doorway. One of her eyes was in darkness; the other saw Morpeth still hesitating in the gleaming world of Ithrea.

'Are you sure?' she said. 'Morpeth, are you *sure?*

'Yes,' he said. 'No. Yes – I mean – oh—' He shoved her inside the doorway.

Rachel blinked. Dust hung thickly in the air, making it difficult to see. Her dad sat on the floor, his head in his hands, an axe at his feet. He glanced slowly upward and when his gaze met hers he broke into tears of relief.

'I thought you—' he stumbled, trying to find the words. 'You were in the wall. I thought—'

Rachel hugged him. When she looked at him again, her many-coloured eyes shone brightly.

'You're different,' he said. 'You've *changed.*'

Rachel kissed him. 'Everything has changed.'

'Where's Eric?'

'He's coming,' Rachel said. 'In fact, he's not the only one coming.'

'Rachel, what do you mean?'

'I mean—'

But there was no holding them back. Scorpa padded, prapsies hopped, Ronnocoden flapped . . . and Morpeth and Eric, dragging the worms as best they could, walked through the doorway.

THE
SCENT OF
MAGIC

BOOK TWO OF
THE DOOMSPELL TRILOGY

'A spellbinding read full of excitement
and suspense.' *Cool Reads*

Chapter 1

eyes

'Rachel, wake up, get out of the dream!' Morpeth shook her gently, then more roughly when she did not move. 'Come on, wake up!'

'What?' Rachel's eyes half-opened.

Briefly Morpeth saw the remains of her nightmare. It dug into her cheek, as big as a dog: the gnarled black claw of a Witch. As Morpeth watched the thick green fingernails faded on Rachel's pale face.

'It's all right,' he said hastily, gripping her shoulders. 'Don't be afraid. You're safe, at home, in your room. There's no Witch.'

Rachel jerked awake and sat up, her breath coming in hurried gasps.

'Oh, Morpeth,' she murmured, '*never* wake me up like that. When I'm dreaming... I might... I could have hurt you.' She buried her face in a pillow, waiting until the cold jagged sensation of the fingernails had gone. 'You should know better,' she said at last. 'A spell might have slipped out.'

'Would you rather your mum faced those claws?' he answered. 'At least I can recognize them.'

Rachel nodded bleakly. 'But it's dangerous, even for you. Always let me wake up naturally, when I'm ready.'

Morpeth grunted, pointing at the sunlight filtering through the curtains. 'I waited as long as I could. Half the day's gone, and your mum was just about to get you up.' He picked a few strands of weed from her hair. 'Interesting smell these have.'

'Oh no,' groaned Rachel, noticing the staleness for the first time. 'I was in the pond again last night, wasn't I?'

'I'm afraid so.'

Rachel bit her lip. 'That's twice this week.'

'Three times.'

'I suppose I had the gills?'

'Yes, the usual scarlet ones, on your neck.'

'Ugh!' Rachel felt below her ears in disgust. 'How long was I under the water this time?'

'About an hour.'

'An *hour*!' Rachel shook her head grimly. 'Then it's getting worse. All right, I'm up.' She listened for a second. 'Will you check the corridor and bathroom are clear?'

Morpeth nipped out, returning moments later. 'Nobody about, and here's a couple of fresh towels. I'll stuff last night's sheets in the wash, shall I?'

Rachel smiled, taking the towels. 'Morpeth, you're my guardian angel.'

Slipping quietly into the bathroom, she used a long hot shower to remove the stink of the pond. Returning to her room, she sat beside the dressing-table mirror, half-heartedly brushing out her long straight dark hair.

Then she stopped. She put the brush down. She turned slowly to the mirror and examined her slim, lightly freckled face.

The eyes that gazed back were no longer quite human. Her old hazel-green eyes, matching her dad's, had gone. Replacing them were her new magical eyes. Spells clustered in the corners, behind the lids. They liked it there, where they could look out onto the world. Throughout the day they crowded forward, eager for her attention. Each spell had its own unique colour. Yesterday's spell-colours had started off scarlet and gold, surrounding her black pupil. This morning there was no pupil at all. There was only a deep wide blue in both eyes, the shade of a summer sky. Rachel had seen that colour many times recently. It was the colour of a flying spell, aching to be used.

Staring at her reflection in the mirror, Rachel said, 'No. I won't fly. I made a promise, I'm keeping it. I won't give in to you!'

'Give in to who?' asked a voice.

Rachel turned, startled. Her mum stood behind her, staring anxiously into the mirror.

'Mum, where did you come from?'

'I've been here awhile, just watching you. And *them*.' Mum studied Rachel's spell-drenched eyes. Their colour had now changed to a mournful grey. 'Those spells,' Mum said angrily. 'What are they expecting from you? Why won't they just leave you in peace for once?'

3

'It's all right, Mum,' Rachel mumbled vaguely. 'I'm ... I'm still in charge of them.'

Mum wrapped her arms around Rachel's neck. Holding her tight, she said in the softest of voices, 'Then tell me why you're trembling? Do you think after twelve years I can't tell when my own daughter's hurting?'

A single tear rolled down Rachel's cheek. She tried to dash the wetness away.

'Let it out,' Mum said. 'You cry it out. Those terrible spells. How dare they do anything to harm you!'

For a few minutes Rachel leaned back into her mother's embrace. Finally she said, 'I'm all right, really I am. I'm fine. I am.'

Mum squeezed Rachel again and simply stood there, obviously reluctant to leave.

'You won't keep staring in that mirror?'

'No more staring today,' Rachel answered, forcing a smile. 'Promise.' As Mum walked slowly to the door, she said, 'You're missing Dad, aren't you?'

Mum halted at the door. 'Is it that obvious?'

'Only because I miss him too. I hate it when he's away.'

'His last foreign contract this year's nearly finished,' Mum told her. 'He'll be back in a month or so.'

'Thirty-eight days,' Rachel said.

Mum smiled conspiratorially. 'So we both count!' She turned to leave. 'Hurry down, will you? I've had just about enough of Eric and the prapsies today. I do love your brother, but he's nine going on six half the time, the things he teaches those child-birds.' She tramped back downstairs, muttering all the way.

4

Rachel finished dressing and made her way to the kitchen. As soon as she entered the prapsies covered their faces.

'Lock away your sparky eyes!' one shrieked, glimpsing her.

Oops, Rachel thought, quickly switching the glowing spell-colours off.

The other prapsy flapped irritably in front of her face. 'Eric could have been blinded!' it squeaked. 'His handsome face could have eye-holes burned in it!'

Rachel knew better than to react in any way. She put some bread on the grill and watched it brown, as if toasting bread fascinated her.

The prapsies hovered next to her nose, pulling faces. They were odd, mixed-up things, the joke creation of a Witch who had once used them as messengers. Bodily they were identical to crows, with the typical sleek, blue-black feathers. But instead of beaks they had noses; and instead of bird-faces, theirs were plump, dimpled and rosy-cheeked, with soft lips. Each prapsy had the head of a baby.

Mum swished by, waving the child-birds out of her way. They parted, then came back together, hovering perfectly over Rachel's head. One blew a raspberry; the other accidentally dribbled on her toast.

'How delightful,' Rachel said, throwing the slice in the bin. 'I wish I knew how they grew their baby-faces back again. I preferred it when they just squawked.'

Both prapsies showed her their toothless gums.

'Gaze at us, chimp face!' they cooed. 'We're so gorgeous. We're so beautiful! Ask Eric.'

Eric sat nearby at the kitchen table, casually turning the pages of a comic.

'You all right, sis?' he asked, glancing up. 'Enjoying the boys' company?'

'I'm fine,' she said dryly. 'But I'd prefer not to be within kissing distance. Do you think you might call the boys off long enough for me to butter my toast?'

'Sure thing.' He whistled.

Instantly both prapsies flew onto his shoulders. They perched there, scowling at Rachel.

'And shut them up for ten minutes,' Mum said in her deadliest voice. 'Or it's crow stew tonight.'

Eric pretended not to hear, but he did finger-zip his mouth. The prapsies sucked their lips in tight to prevent any more insults escaping.

Eric was a short stocky boy with a tough expression he often practised. His most striking feature was his hair – a blond mass of curls. Eric hated his hair. Mothers liked to touch the soft waviness of it. In a couple of years he was determined to get the locks hacked off. A skinhead. For now he had to be content with the prapsies messing it up as often as possible with their claws.

'I suppose the prapsies *slept* with you again last night?' Rachel said witheringly.

'Of course.' Eric grinned – and so did the prapsies – imitating him with eerie precision.

'I've watched them,' Rachel went on. 'They sit on your bed, with those big baby eyes. It's spooky. They copy everything you do. When you turn, they turn. They even imitate your snoring.'

'Ah, it's true,' Eric chuckled, 'They adore me.' He clicked his fingers. One prapsy immediately nudged the page of his comic over with its small upturned nose.

'Pathetic,' Rachel muttered. 'Three morons. Where's Morpeth?'

'I could tell you,' Eric replied. 'But what's in it for me?'

'He's in the garden,' Mum said, clipping Eric round the ear. She handed Rachel some freshly buttered toast. 'Eat a crust before you go out, won't you?'

After breakfast Rachel wandered into the back garden. It was a bakingly hot July day, with almost all of the summer holidays still left. Morpeth lay spread out by the pond. He was a thin boy, with startlingly blue eyes and thick sandy hair sticking out in all directions. An ice-cool drink lay within easy reach of his bronze arm.

Rachel smiled affectionately. 'I see you've settled in for the summer.'

'Thanks to Dragwena, I missed out on several hundred summers,' Morpeth said. 'I'm catching up as best I can.' He pulled a can of coke out of the pond and handed it to Rachel. 'I've been saving this. How are you feeling?'

'Pretty grim,' she said, easing into the garden hammock.

'You certainly smell better. I suppose you scrubbed with soap?'

'Yes, Morpeth, I did,' Rachel said, laughing. 'Why? Don't you?'

'Still can't stand the slimy feel,' he admitted. 'That funny sweet smell too, there's something wrong about it. Of course, we didn't have soap when I was a boy. Everyone smelt awful and no one cared a bit.'

7

Rachel couldn't quite get used to this new child-Morpeth. She had met him a year before on another world: Ithrea. Rachel shuddered even now to think of that desolate world of dark snow. A hated Witch, Dragwena, had ruled there. Morpeth had been her reluctant servant.

For centuries he had been forced to watch as Dragwena abducted children from our world. Rachel and Eric were the last to be kidnapped. When she arrived, Rachel discovered that all children possess magic they cannot use on Earth. That was why the Witch wanted them – to serve her own purposes. Morpeth had tutored Rachel, and she blossomed, discovering that she was more magically gifted than any child who had come before – the first strong enough to truly resist Dragwena. Eric, too, had a gift, and this time it was one no other child possessed. Uniquely, he could unmake spells. He could *destroy* them. In a final terrifying battle Rachel and Eric had fought the Witch's Doomspell and witnessed the death of Dragwena at the hands of the great Wizard, Larpskendya.

As Rachel gazed at Morpeth now, it was difficult for her to remember that for hundreds of years he had been a wrinkled old man kept alive only by the Witch's magic. Somehow he had defied the worst of Dragwena's influence, and when Rachel and Eric arrived he risked his life over and over for them. In gratitude, the Wizard Larpskendya gave Morpeth back all the lost years of childhood Dragwena had taken from him. He returned, as a boy, home – but not his own home. His original family were long dead, of course. So Rachel's parents had secretly adopted him – and here he was, a year later, a man-boy in a summer garden. A few other creatures had chosen to return from Ithrea with Rachel and Eric. Only the prapsies remained. The wolf-cub, Scorpa, Ronnocoden the eagle, and a few worms, had soon disappeared, deciding to make a new life amongst their own kind on Earth.

'What's wrong?' Rachel asked, noticing that Morpeth looked slightly uncomfortable.

'It's these shorts,' he pouted. 'Your mum forgets that I'm five-hundred-and-thirty-seven years old. I don't *like* stripy pants.'

'You couldn't wear your old leathers from Ithrea forever, Morpeth. You've outgrown them.'

'But they *felt* good,' he said. 'These shorts just look stupid. They don't fit properly, either. Your mum always assumes I'm the same size as Eric.'

'Are they too tight?'

'Too loose,' Morpeth said meaningfully.

'Mm. Dangerous.' Rachel smiled. 'Must tell Mum about that … of course, you could go to the shops and buy your own.'

Morpeth gave her a grouchy shrug. Shopping meant setting foot out of the house and across the dreaded street. Traffic unnerved him. There had been no cars when he was a boy, or aeroplanes. The sheer *noisiness* of modern life made him constantly edgy, and he avoided roads whenever possible.

For a few minutes Rachel lay in the hammock next to the pond, simply enjoying the sunshine and the light breeze blowing over her legs.

'Morpeth,' she said at last, 'I was in bed for fifteen hours last night. I can't wake up. These things my spells are doing while I'm asleep ... what's happening?'

'You know the answer to that,' he said bluntly.

Rachel shook her head. 'I know my spells want to be used,' she said. 'But they've behaved until now. What's changed? Why are they suddenly taking over like this?'

'They're defying you,' he answered. 'They're restless, impatient. Magic isn't something you can just tame like a pet, Rachel. Especially *your* magic.' He leant across and tapped her head. 'Your spells are far too intense, too ambitious, to leave you alone for long. And you stopped listening to their requests months ago, didn't you? You locked them out completely.'

'I had to,' Rachel protested. 'They were too tempting. Larpskendya made me promise not to use my spells—'

'I know,' Morpeth said. 'But your spells don't care about a promise made to a Wizard. They don't like being ignored. You won't listen while you're awake, so they come out to play at night – when they can take charge of your dreams.'

Rachel bent across to stir the surface of the pond. 'But why dump me under water?'

'Why not?' Morpeth said. 'Water must be an interesting place for bored spells to experiment. There's the challenge of how to enable you to breathe without lungs. And how to enable you to inhale water without damaging your body. Those things are difficult. They require many intricate spells, co-operating closely.'

Rachel thought of the gills. 'I can handle them,' she

insisted. 'Larpskendya warned me a party of Witches could detect my spells, even from space. That might lead the Witches to all children. I won't break my promise!'

'You already *have*,' snorted Morpeth. He stood up. 'You must take back control, Rachel. Give your spells something to do – room to breathe at least. And do it while you're awake, and you can restrain them.'

'Nothing terrible's happened yet...'

Morpeth met her gaze. 'Are you going to wait until it does? I know you wouldn't strike out deliberately, Rachel, but what about your nightmares? What if your mum tried to wake you at the wrong time? This morning, for instance. Anything could have occurred. I saw the claw.' He stared earnestly at her. 'That's your worst nightmare, isn't it? And mine too: in my darkest dreams I'm facing Dragwena again. I'm hunted by a Witch.'

Rachel shivered. She tried never to think of Dragwena.

Bringing the drink of Coke to her lips, she noticed a wasp. It buzzed around the lid of the can, crawled under the tab and finally fell into the drink. Rachel sighed, absently tipping the wasp onto the grass.

'What spells just came into your head?' Morpeth asked sharply.

'Only the usual ones.'

'Such as?'

'Four spells: one to kill the wasp; a second to rescue it; a third to disinfect the can.' She watched the wasp, wings fizzing, stagger across the lawn, and smiled. 'And a warming spell to dry the insect's wings.'

'Which spell came first to mind?'

The killing spell, thought Rachel, and Morpeth read the answer in her face.

'I wouldn't have hurt the wasp,' she told him.

'I know,' said Morpeth. 'But it's interesting that the most dangerous spells offer themselves first. They always dominate the others.'

Rachel leaned over the pond and gazed at her reflection. Her eyes had turned a deep brown, like moistened sand. She looked for more vibrant colours, but her spells were unusually reticent – as if they did not want her spying on them. Why should that be?

For the first time in months Rachel turned her attention inward. What are you up to? she demanded. Several spells became silent, tucking themselves slyly away, not wishing her to recognize the mischief they planned.

They're waiting, Rachel realized – waiting until I fall asleep.

To Morpeth, she said, 'You'd better keep a close eye on me tonight.'

Don't miss the next exciting book in

THE DOOMSPELL TRILOGY

Rachel and her brother, Eric, are extraordinary.
She is a spell-maker. He is a destroyer of spells.

The high Witch, Heebra, wants Rachel and Eric
crushed and her enemies, the Wizards, killed.
A party of Witches is dispatched to find the
thousands of children with powers like Rachel's,
and turn them into a ferocious army.

Can Rachel and Eric stop the Witches and win
the battle between good and evil?

The final gripping instalment

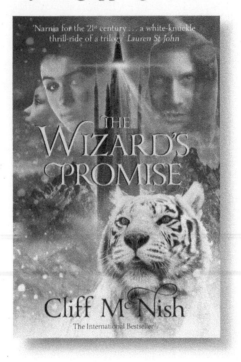

'Narnia for the 21st century... a white-knuckle
thrill-ride of a trilogy' Lauren St John

THE
WIZARD'S
PROMISE

Cliff McNish

The International Bestseller

The magic of all children has been released.
Now, throughout the skies of Earth they fly,
playing the deadly spell-games.

Only Rachel watches for what she knows is
coming – the invasion of the Witches. And this
time there is a new enemy – the terrifying Gridda-
breed. Rachel and Eric will need all their skill and
courage in the coming battle – knowing that if
they fail, the whole world will
be engulfed in darkness.

THE DOOMSPELL TRILOGY
So far, translated into 26 languages

Cliff McNish is acclaimed as 'one of our most talented thriller writers' (*The Times*) and has written numerous novels for teenagers and children. His debut fantasy series – *The Doomspell Trilogy* – hailed him as a 'great new voice in writing for children' (*The Bookseller*), and has been published in twenty-six languages worldwide. His multiple-award winning *Breathe: A Ghost Story* was voted in May 2013 as one of the top 100 adult and children's novels of all time by The Schools Network of British Librarians.

Cliff actively works to promote creative writing, performing a variety of talks and workshops in schools, libraries, reading clubs and book festivals.

To find out more about Cliff McNish's award-winning books go to **www.cliffmcnish.com**